T0208277

DEDICATION

To My Mother

THE X-MEX

Short stories of Mystery and Suspense.

Gino Briseno

Order this book online at www.trafford.com
or email orders@trafford.com

Cover Design by Michael A. Briseno

Most Trafford titles are also available at major online book retailers.

© Copyright 2011 Gino Briseno.
All rights reserved. No part of this publication may be reproduced, stored in a retrieval
system, or transmitted, in any form or by any means, electronic, mechanical, photocopying,
recording, or otherwise, without the written prior permission of the author.

Printed in the United States of America.

ISBN: 978-1-4269-7624-7 (sc)
ISBN: 978-1-4269-7622-3 (hc)
ISBN: 978-1-4269-7627-8 (e)

Library of Congress Control Number: 2011912348

Trafford rev. 07/16/2011

 www.trafford.com

North America & international
toll-free: 1 888 232 4444 (USA & Canada)
phone: 250 383 6864 ♦ fax: 812 355 4082

The following short stories are based in true events. Some names and places have been changed to protect the guilty.

THE VANISHING STALLION

By the time the long and dark shadows of the mountain peaks reached the main trail, we were just beginning to descend into the canyon. Just ahead, past the dry creek, was a narrow passage carved out of the granite wall. This site, known by the locals as "El Paso Del Muerto", The Dead Man Pass, had been the silent witness of a hideous and unspeakable crime.

In the early Eighteenth Century a wealthy man of the region had been ambushed, robbed and killed on this very spot. According to local lore, part of the gold and silver he and his peons were transporting was buried in the surrounding area, but despite countless searches, the treasure had never been found.

Night comes quickly on these mountains. Perhaps the high peaks, narrow valleys and triple canopy forest that cover the slopes have a lot to do with it. When the last dying rays shine on the peaks, dark follows immediately, swallowing everything in its path, no twilight, and with no warning comes complete darkness. Then from their hiding nests and burrows, the creatures of the night come alive. Like miniature neon lights, myriads of fireflies advertise their existence. Chirping crickets and cicadas play hide and seek in the undergrowth and a strong scent of bark, moss and leaves fill the senses. But as the night grows colder, the forest and darkness seem to morph and hide something more sinister.

We had planned to reach our destination just before nightfall. Perhaps overconfident we had rested a little too long at our last stop. However, that was more than an hour ago and I was exhausted, even though our two backpacks were loaded with just the essentials. Two boxes of crackers, a shovel, a pickaxe, one gallon of water, a small bottle of gasoline, two flashlights, two machetes, two lengths of rope, a kerosene lamp, a 38 caliber pistol with five rounds in the mag and a 22 semiautomatic caliber rifle with sixteen rounds of ammo.

As we approached the narrow passage at the bottom of the ravine, now in complete darkness, the flashlight in front of me stopped momentarily. My companion was illuminating the sheer cliff at the edge of the trail.

"El Paso Del Muerto" he said in ominous tone.

"Is this where the treasure is?" I whispered.

"No, just ahead, not far from here," he said pointing with the beam deep into the canyon.

I was having second thoughts about this whole deal.

Everything had started two years before during a trip to this northern Mexican region where I had met my companion.

Victor was a nineteen year old fast talking chap that in some recesses of his obtuse mind believed that, just because he was a couple years older than I was, he had a lot more experience and knowledge than I would ever achieve in my lifetime. There is no doubt he had done a few things, but none that his mother would ever have approved or be proud of. Nonetheless, we became good friends, and one day around the campfire during harvest time, we started discussing ghost stories and buried treasures.

"They say that you see a burning fire coming out from where, supposedly, the treasure is buried." I ventured.

"Only on June the 24th, St. John's Day, and it is a bluish fire." Victor said in a matter of fact tone.

"I think it's all just a bunch of crap, you know, old wives' tales." I said a little annoyed to his know-it-all attitude.

"What makes you say that?" He said turning in my direction, perhaps a little startled to be challenged.

"Well, how many people, you know, have actually dug out a treasure? How many people, you know, have seen a treasure or this... bluish fire? Huh? I bet you none! Zip, zero. You know, the thing with these tales is that there is just no way to verify it because whoever made up these stories is very conveniently dead, gone, six feet under or otherwise deceased. Get it?"

He pulled a long draw on his cigarette and puffs of smoke came with every word. "I saw it." He said slowly.

"You saw what?"

"The fire, the bluish flames from a buried treasure."

"What? Wait, wait a minute! When and where did this happen?"

"A couple of years ago,"

"You're telling me you know where a treasure is and you haven't dug it out yet? Please, you are stretching it too far."

"I swear to God I'm telling you the truth."

"So, what's the problem?"

"Well, is not that I haven't tried." He said with a long face. "I've been looking for a partner, you know, but as soon as I mention the place...is like, they're not interested anymore."

"Why is that so?" I said trying to hide my curiosity.

"First of all," he said in a conspiratorial tone. "I wouldn't go by myself." Then almost in a whisper, "The place is haunted."

"Well, I don't blame them." I figured. "If you believe these silly folk tales, where the Landlords would hire ranch hands or peons to bury the gold then kill them right after and throw them in the pit, so the poor souls were condemned to linger and guard the site. Of course that goes without saying that the landlord would be the only one that knew the treasure location, and who knows, maybe the one responsible for spreading these haunted tales that..."

"I know, I know." He interrupted. "But, this place is not just haunted." He stood up and paced to the edge of the campfire. "You see," he continued gazing into the dark. "I don't mind ghosts, spirits don't scare me and I laugh at the Dead. No, this place is different. It is jinxed, cursed, evil..." He was now looking straight at me over the campfire flames. "I think the place is guarded by Satan himself, and that my friend is where I draw the line, I don't want anything to do with THAT guy."

A cold breeze blew across the valley chilling the very marrow of my bones. The flames of the fire flickered momentarily sending long dancing shadows as if with life of their own.

"So, is this where you saw the fire?"

"Yes, the place is called El Paso Del Muerto."

"Paso Del Muerto? Never heard of it."

"About two years ago I was coming back from Del Rio." he began. "I decided to take the old trail that runs across the canyon, kind of a short cut, if you don't mind the steep slopes. Anyway, I figured I would make it out of the canyon before sunset. Well, no such luck. It was already dark when I was half way down. I know it sounds foolish but I didn't want to backtrack. So I just kept going."

"Did you have a flashlight?"

"Yeah, that's why I wasn't too concerned at that time."

"So, what happened?"

"Down the slope, at the bottom of the canyon and some distance from the trail, I saw this bluish light behind the bushes. At first, I thought people were camping. I stopped and tried to get a better look at it, but there was no noise, no sound and nobody around."

"Was it like a ball of fire up in the air?" Now, I could hardly hide my excitement.

"From where I was, it was only like a glow in the dark. But as I moved closer, it looked like it was coming from the ground like the flame from a gas stove."

"Then, what happened?"

"I started looking for a rock or something to throw at it. But I couldn't find anything, when I looked back, the flame had disappeared! Nothing! Gone!"

"Damn, that must have been scary!"

"No, at that time I didn't think it was anything other than freaky. But as I got back on the trail I realized that just ahead was El Paso del Muerto, and just at that moment I heard the avalanche. Massive chunks of rock breaking off the cliffs high above and crushing down the ravine."

"Holy...!"

"By now I was freaking scared!"

"So, what happened?"

"I remember I stood there frozen, flattened against a rocky wall waiting to be squashed any second. It seemed like an eternity, those rocks smashing and breaking trees on their way down. I could not move. Suddenly at the last second, everything stopped. No noise, no rocks, nothing! I was sweating or so I thought, when I regained my breath I shone the light, I noticed it was blood from cuts and bruises and that I was standing right there at Paso Del Muerto!"

"Are you saying you don't remember walking from where you were to where you ended up?"

"Believe me I've been trying to make sense of it and the only thing I can think of, is the curse of El Muerto. Because when I got home and I told my mom what happened, she said, she wasn't surprised because it was June the 24th and Don Abundio, Satan himself or both, were on the loose."

"I think you better tell me what you know about Don Abundio from the beginning because now I'm getting more confused by the minute."

"Well, it is a long story."

"I'm all ears."

"According to legend, early in the 18th century, all this land belonged to one man, Don Abundio Mar. He was a wealthy, but cruel and despot, Landlord that ruled the hacienda with an iron fist.

One day Don Abundio was returning from Jalpan, a town up north, with mules and donkeys loaded with gold and silver coins. The profits were from the sale of some of his extensive herds grazing the valleys. Don Abundio and three peons were ambushed and killed just as they reached the narrow passage in the canyon.

Three badly decomposed bodies were found days later at the bottom of the ravine. But the gold and silver had mysteriously disappeared.

Most accounts agree up to this point, however, what happened next depends on who tells the story. One version goes something like this. Individual remains could not be identified and those half-eaten bones left by the coyotes were scattered down the cliff. After all, according to some accounts, Don Abundio used to dress just like his raggedy peons. Others say that only Don Abundio's skull was recovered.

The thieves then buried all the loot in the surrounding area, planning to return for it when things calmed down. But they never did because they killed each other out of greed and fear.

In another version, the thieves kill the peons, take Don Abundio elsewhere in the surrounding area, kill him and bury part of the loot with his body. Because they could not carry all the loot, the thieves were planning to return later to pick up the rest, but never did. Some say they were killed in a brawl-bar while spending the loot.

The funny thing is that most versions of the story agree on what happens next; a closed and sealed coffin, allegedly containing Don Abundio's bones was laid in the Hacienda's main room for the funeral. When dusk came, the coffin was surrounded by vicious vultures that prevented people from getting anywhere near or around it. The superstitious peasants ran terrified out of the hacienda.

The following morning, to their great relief, the peasants found no traces of the vultures, but when they opened the coffin, the bones had vanished!"

"Maybe the vultures ate them" I ventured.

"No, no, the coffin was still nailed shut when they opened it."

"So what happened with the bones?"

"That's the second part of the story. But at this point, fearful of even an empty casket, the peasants, sworn to secrecy, filled it with rocks and buried it in the local cemetery."

A distant howling beyond the hills was followed by an apprehensive barking downwind from a stray dog. Victor paused for a moment.

"Long before his death," he finally said. "There were rumors that Don Abundio had a pact with the Devil." He paused for a moment to gauge my reaction.

"Wow, now the plot thickens!" I said trying to hide my fear.

"He was seen," he continued, "about every month or so, going into this cave, inhabited by a pitch-black bull. Don Abundio would then be swallowed by this bull-like monster and then defecated the following day." Victor took a long deep draw from his smoldering cigarette," a freaking and disgusting price to pay but without a doubt part of the deal."

"Why he had to do this?"

"It was a pact; Don Abundio..." He said in more commanding tone. "had been given fabulous wealth in exchange for his worthless Soul.

When he died the Devil came to claim not just his Soul but his body as well."

"You mean the bones…"

"Yes, the vultures took the remains to the depths of Hell."

For a moment I almost expected Victor to turn around and with a smile in his face say something silly like, he was just pulling my leg, or making up the story. When he didn't, I said with pun intended. "Now, that's a Hell of a tale."

"And as far as I know it is all true." He said ignoring my cue, and letting out a long puff of smoke.

"Okay, let's see." I said trying to make sense of it. "This fire that you saw was from the treasure stolen from Don Abundio, I presume."

"Part of the treasure, but yes, you presume correctly my Dear Watson." He said in his best clipped British imitation.

"Well, seems like we have a problem my Dear Holmes." I said imitating his imitation.

"What's that?"

"Why would the Devil be guarding the treasure?"

"Why? Two reasons, one; the money is still legally His. You know the pact, contract, etc."

"Okay, you got me on that one. What's number two?"

"The Devil got kind of cheated out of the deal."

"Cheated? Wow! That would be a first one."

"No, really. The Devil never actually got the entire body. Remember, only some of the remains were found, some were eaten by coyotes, some put in the coffin, and some buried with the treasure. Now this is what I think happened, I'm just throwing my two cents into the legend but I think it is entirely possible. As we all know, in all transactions with the Devil legal or otherwise, the Soul is the commodity but he also claims the body as well, why? I don't know."

"Hey, who knows, maybe he has a thing for the bodies," I said trying to light up the subject.

"I don't think that's funny." He said with what I thought was a hint of annoyance.

"For Christ sake! What kind of self-respectable Devil lets the cayos beat him to chow time?"

"I think you're being a little disrespectful." He said now with more clearly defined annoyance. I was taken aback momentarily, this guy actually believed everything he was telling me!"

"Okay, never mind. So, are you saying that the Devil is not only guarding the treasure but wants to recover the rest of the body?"

"Exacto Mondo." He said with visible relief."

"So, if we unearth these remains and…" I was starting to see the picture.

"Exactly." He interrupted. "We would be basically helping Him get what he wants. So in theory, we should fear no evil, and of course, the treasure would be our reward!"

"How much do you think is the treasure worth?"

"I have no Idea but I figure at least a sack full of gold and silver coins. Worth thousands and thousands of pesos, more than you can imagine." His hands were moving through imaginary piles of money.

"Well I can imagine a lot." I said with pesos signs in my eyes.

The flashlight beam was now illuminating a group of trees and bushes forming a semicircle just off the trail. Tall grass and rocks piled on the edge, forced us to give a wide berth to reach the clearing, or so I thought. "Better this way." Victor said in a whisper. "We don't want to leave any fresh tracks. Also keep your voice down, these canyon walls act like a freaking amplifier." He said as we reached a clearing in the bushes.

"You said that by coming at night we wouldn't have to worry about people snooping around." I said as I lowered my backpack on an old fallen tree.

"I said it was less likely." He said still panting.

"OK, where exactly did you see the fire?"

He got up and did a sweep with his flashlight of the surrounding bushes, then a quick scan back and forth from the trees to the trail, as if recalling some mental distance. "Right here," he said shining the light next to a thorny bush.

Flashlight in hand I started inspecting the site shoving and pulling weeds. The place to say the least was unremarkable.

"Don't look like a burial place to me." I said with a hint of disappointment.

"What were you expecting?" He was trying to get the kerosene lamp going. "A big neon sign reading TREASURE: DIG HERE?" He said with a chuckle.

"Hey, that would've been nice too. What I'm talking about is, maybe a mound of dirt or a pile of rocks, something like that, you know."

"Same difference, why do you think nobody has found it yet after all these years? They have been digging in the wrong places. After all, two hundred years can wipe out pretty much all traces."

After we had rested a little to regain our breath, we cleared an area the size of a large room. Then we started digging exploration holes until we found a likely spot were the dirt appeared to have been disturbed in the past.

"Right here," Victor said.

It must have been past midnight. It was hard to tell. Through the triple canopy, we could barely see a slice of the sky and the dim glow of the moon had vanished behind the jagged peaks of the canyon. We had taken turns digging and going to the lookout post, my eyes trying to get used to the dark, again. I stared up and down the trail into pitch-blackness. My hearing now attuned to the sounds of the jungle. The "thud, thud" of the pickaxe back in the pit and the cacophony of the cicadas were broken now and then by the far howling of a lone wolf. Victor had mentioned that sounds were carried very far in the canyon. I hoped he was right. Because the wolf sounded awfully close. I held my rifle closer and moved a cartridge into the firing chamber. I didn't want to take any chances.

I figured we had at least four more hours of safe digging before any traveler would venture down this canyon. Nonetheless, we took turns at the pit and at the same time kept a wary eye on the trail. Twice we had stopped and turned the lantern off. The first time, a noise in the bushes turned out to be an armadillo that ran as scared as we were and disappeared across the trail. The second time was a raspy noise down the trail and although we waited a good while it did not repeat. Victor thought it was armadillo number two, I wasn't too sure.

The "thud, thud," had stopped and gone quiet for a while, I climbed down from the rocky outcrop with one eye closed to retain my night vision just in case I had to stay, but as I looked in the pit's direction, Victor was climbing out. "Bye, bye night vision." I muttered out as I returned to the pit.

Shirtless and drenched in sweat he was now shoveling away the mound of dirt and gravel accumulated at the edge of the pit.

"Anything?" I said looking down into the pit.

"No" he said shaking his head.

The pit had grown considerable deeper and wider, about a shovel length wide, maybe two in length and chest high deep with one-side part ramp and part steps. This was backbreaking work. Were we digging in the right place? Was there any treasure at all? I gave him the hand signal for break and time out as I walked past the edge of the pit to where the backpacks were leaning up against the trunk of an old tree. I heard him throw the shovel back in the pit as I hung up my rifle, machete and hat from a branch. I laid my flashlight on top of the backpack and went down the ramp.

"Don't dig this way anymore." He said tapping the spot he was standing on. "But keep breaking on that side where the dirt feels softer."

"What about that side?" I asked.

"No, I don't think we have to." He held the kerosene lantern, adjusted the flame, set it down on the edge of the pit, grabbed his canteen and disappeared in the direction of the lookout post.

I had been digging for some time now. Just a narrow trench off the center of the pit and now the whole thing looked like a big "T". To my delight, the dirt on this side was a lot easier to break and I was making good progress, when something in the soil caught my attention. I was breaking through a layer of reddish and rusty soil. Closer inspection revealed what appeared to be bits and pieces of wood, but I could not tell whether it was just an old root or something else. Excitedly I started probing deeply. The pickaxe hit something hard just below the surface, something flat and wider than just a root.

"Damn this is it!" I said out loud.

Now on my hands and knees I started clearing the spot.

"What is it?" A voice said from above the pit.

I jumped out of my skin. "Oh! You son of… you scared the hell…" I looked up, but the lantern by the edge of the pit was glaring right in my face and I could only see a blurry shadow behind it. I was about to jump up and down and yell "We found it! We found it!" But something in that shadow at the last moment made me change my mind. For an instant, like a revelation, I knew that if that treasure was there I would not live to see it. Shading the light from my eyes, I could see the shadow standing on the edge of the pit and the rifle pointing in my direction.

"I just hit some big rocks," I said nonchalant. "I don't think there is anything here."

Ignoring that rifle and playing dumb wasn't going to buy me much time. My heartbeat had switched to overdrive. "Think, think," I kept telling myself. "You got to keep talking." But my mouth was dry and no words would come out.

Then it hit me, now I understood his plan. What a sucker I was! He had to deliver somebody, anybody, a soul in exchange for the gold! And I had fallen for it.

Suddenly I did not want any treasure. "Please God" I started praying. "If I get out of this one, I promise I don't want to be rich. I promise to be a happy poor farmer." The void in the pit of my stomach was painfully spreading. I had to get a grip of myself. For some unknown reason of all the thoughts racing thru my mind one came loud and clear "Do not show your fear, think, think, you must control your fear."

The words were resonating as clear as if it was yesterday. For a fraction of a second, I was transported eight years back in time.

I must have been eight years old at that time. My dad and I had walked for miles through the jungle to see this Indian. I don't recall why we were going to see him but the one thing I'm sure is that I was scared.

We were still far from his house when the faint faraway barking started. "They picked us up." My dad said as he pulled his machete out, cut a branch from a tree and made two sticks the length of a baseball bat. "Just remember," he said, as he handed me the smaller one. "No matter what happens, stay with me, don't run away."

The barking was growing louder and closer, they were racing to meet the intruders.

The narrow trail was barely visible under the overgrowth, sneaking around massive tree trunks and jagged rocks covered with thick green foliage. High above the tree tops only thin pencils of light came breaking through the canopy.

The dogs were closer, much closer. They would appear any second out of the bend on the trail. "Stay against the rock and don't run. Don't show your fear. A dog will sense your fear and attack. The worst thing to do is run, don't do it." My dad said as we readied for battle. The intense fear of impending doom was indescribable. The panic screams in your mind and your body wants to run for your life.

Just then, a pack of six howling jaws exploded out of the bend, bared teeth dripping in the heat of the attack and trying to outrace each other. My instinct was yelling at me "run, run." But just before I sprinted, my dad's hand was on my shoulder, "stay still," he yelled over the deafening noise.

We were quickly surrounded.

A beast-like demon lunged for my flesh and met my stick that I kept swinging to keep it at bay, I could see one trying to climb the rock to attack from the rear, and the semicircle was closing. Soon another one clenched my stick and would not let go. My Dad was swinging at three or four ganged up on him. Then out of the corner of my eye I saw a blur of teeth and claws flying in my direction, then "Kapoom!" my father had caught him in midflight with a solid swing and dropped him to the ground. The dog gave out a long and painful squeal and retreated whimpering. This paralyzed momentarily the rest of the pack including the one wrestling my stick to which I was still locked in a deadly tug of war. Amazingly all, at once, turned around and flew the scene in hastily retreat from whence they came.

Back in the trench, I had to think. I had to control my fear. The kerosene lantern… yes that was it… all I had to do was get to it fast… no he was standing too close to it. Running was out of the question, I was a sitting duck. I had to talk my way out of this. "Look…" I started to say, but the words just wouldn't come out. My attention was now fixated to that rifle that now was coming up slowly into a firing position. I wanted to run, but I couldn't move. My legs were paralyzed weighing a ton and felt sinking into the ground.

Just at that moment, a far and faint noise up the trail made us turn simultaneously. "Thank God someone's coming." I thought. I felt myself regain control of my body. It was now or never, I lunged for the lantern, and I saw his shadow do the same, but my feet were sinking in the dirt and by the time I reached the edge Victor had it already and was turning it off.

Now it was pitch dark and none of us said anything. I knew he still had the rifle but it was less likely to shoot me if somebody was coming. I ran back to the other side of the trench and up the ramp. I could not see anything, but just trying to remember where everything was. I fell and rolled over loose dirt and bushes.

"Hey" I heard him calling, the voice still coming from the far side of the pit. "Nice try son of…" I thought, as I stood still but trying to orient myself and find the backpacks. I crawled on all fours and in what felt like a long time I was then by the backpacks. Flashlight was there but I didn't want to turn it on. Quickly, I pulled out the handgun. "Thank God it's here." Now I felt much better as I moved a shell into the chamber and removed the safety lock in one swift motion. "Okay you son of a gun what were you saying?" I muted to myself and aimed into the dark. As I fanned out my arm I hit something hanging just above the next backpack. I almost pulled the trigger. I felt it. I could not believe it, it was the rifle, just where I had left it earlier!

"Hey." The voice was now closer but in hushed tones. I moved the safety lock back on and slid the gun in the small of my back. I grabbed the flashlight and shined it in his direction. He was coming my way with a shovel in his hand. Maybe I was hallucinating, something very strange was happening. I didn't know what it was. Maybe I was seeing things.

"What the hell you think you're doing. Shut the fucking light off!"

I quickly turned the flashlight off and made sure I had the rifle on my side, at the same time trying to make sense of it all. He sat next to me. "You didn't have to run." he said in a whisper. "Whoever is coming down is still far up the slope. You scared me, because when I turned the light off you took off like a maniac fumbling in the dark." I was surprised he sounded genuinely concerned, but I was still in shock.

"Hey. I'm talking to you, are you all right?"

"Yeah, yeah," I finally said trying to sound casual. "I thought someone was coming and I got scared and…"

"Shhh!" He interrupted. "Hear that?" Now the noise was closer and distinct. A rider, the horseshoes striking the loose gravel, sliding and regaining hold on the steep slope, yes, I could hear it.

"Let's go to the lookout post, maybe we can see who he is." Victor said.

I got up and realized my knee hurt a little, I grabbed my rifle, I wasn't going to trust my own shadow. Plus I needed a walking cane. As we walked to the lookout post I almost confided to Victor what I had seen, but after a quick consideration I changed my mind. For one, it all could have been just a trick of light and shadows, but then I wasn't going to give him any ideas.

The lookout post was an outcrop of rocks and bushes where one could dominate a good part of the trail without been seen. The side of the trail going uphill was framed by massive boulders, and then farther away took a sharp turn into what was the entrance to the Dead Man Pass. In front of us was a good stretch of dirt and gravel, then the trail meandered in lazy bends and disappeared down the canyon. Not that we could see anything now, we were assuming the rider carried a light.

The sound of the raider was now so clear we could not only hear the huffing and puffing of the horse, but also the sense of urgency of the horseman, the leather rubbing of the stirrups and the tinkling of the spurs hugging the stallion.

We started into pitch-blackness, our eyes trying to adjust.

The horseman was now crossing the Dead Man Pass. Its pace quickened as it came into the open stretch, the noise was almost deafening in front of us...

Then, nothing!

The horseman had vanished! My mind was trying to make sense of it. "He never went past us. Maybe he's standing right there and is looking right at us!" The hair on the nape of my neck froze and a chill ran through my bones. But wait... there was no noise from the horse, and then I realized there was no noise period! No crickets, no birds, no nothing!

Just dead silence!

My heart was beating so hard I thought it would give us away! I wanted to say a prayer but my mind was blank and I just kept thinking "Oh God! Oh God!" I stood there motionless for what seemed like a long time, my eyes closed and clutching my rifle.

A hand grabbed my shoulder. I totally freaked out and let out a scream that was probably heard for miles.

"It's me!" Victor said shining the light on his face.

I then let out a scream even louder.

"Shut the fuck up!" he said not the least amused. "You want to let everybody know we're here?" He said as he swept the trail up and down with the light beam.

"Where the hell did he go?"

"I have no idea. Let's get the hell out of here!" I was still shaking.

"Wait! Maybe that was a good sign. Maybe we are close to the treasure… and didn't you mention something…?"

"No. I didn't see or mention anything, and I don't want any treasure." But he was already running back to the pit.

"Hey, wait for me!"

By the time I caught up with him he had the lantern lit and was jumping into the pit.

"Wait! Are you out of your freaking mind? You want to keep digging after all this?"

"Don't be a stupid chicken. The treasure must be here!" He was now in a frenzy digging where I had left off.

"I'm leaving right now!" I said. "If you want to stay, stay. That *thing* or whatever it was could be anywhere and when it comes back I don't want to be around." I grabbed my backpack and started out.

I stopped at the edge of the illuminated circle. "Come on, let's go" I didn't want to venture by myself into the dark. I turned around and noticed he was digging on the same spot I had struck the object. I just sat there and watched. He was going to hit it any second, but he kept digging and digging. He went past the one foot mark, then two feet and still nothing!

What happened with the solid wood I felt or whatever it was? Oh my God! This was freaking madness!

"I told you there is nothing!" I said with relief, but I could see his frustration growing as he kept digging.

Finally, he threw the shovel and lay down on the loose dirt exhausted. He stood there on his back with arms outstretched and started cursing the devil, the ghosts and whatever spirits were hiding "his" treasure.

The wind blowing up the ravine was howling through the cliffs. That's when I noticed the sounds of the jungle again, the chirp of the crickets the hooter of the owls but also, something else, the howling of the lone wolf, and this time closer, much closer.

Hurriedly Victor got out of the pit. "Let's go, let's go." He said as he started picking up his stuff.

I helped him pack up and after making sure we did not leave anything behind we headed out for the trail. We stopped shortly at the spot where the Horseman had disappeared. "I don't want to get a nasty surprise from that stupid wolf." Victor said, sweeping the flat stretch up and down with the light beam. I did the same but I wasn't looking for the wolf. I was still too terrified to even mention it.

Time had ceased to exist and I really didn't care. All I wanted to do was to get out of Dodge and fast, but first we had to go through the dreadful Pass. Concentrated only on the front beam of the flashlight and not brave enough to even look sideways, or worse, behind us where every shade and shadow from the tree branches gave the impression of gigantic long fingers reaching over the path. We crossed El Paso del Muerto in stoned silence. I don't know about Victor but I was busy machine-gunning Hail Mary's like crazy.

We did not exchange words during the uphill trek. We were gasping for air and small talk was out of the question. But mainly because we knew that as long as we remained in the canyon, we were still under the spell of the curse or whatever it was in the woods.

Once we were over the ridge and a little way on the other side of the canyon we felt a great sense of relief. But best of all, breaking through the tree tops was first light. We tossed our backpacks on the ground and lay down to regain our breath. With the courage and assurance that only daylight can bring we felt as if we had come out of a tunnel, out of some unreal dimension of ghosts, light and shadows.

"What the hell do you think it was?"

"Which one?" Victor said without missing a beat.

"The Horseman, what else?"

"The Horseman was one, but just before that, there was The Shadow." He was drinking the last from his canteen and I could see his hands shaking.

"What Shadow are you talking about? I didn't see anything." I was starting to worry.

"See, I didn't want to scare you."

"Well, it's too late now, so spit it out."

"When I was at the lookout post I heard you were saying something in the pit. So I went over to see what was happening, I thought you were calling me or something, and just before I got over there I saw a shadow by the edge of the pit, and you were talking to it! As I came closer, it disappeared. That is when I heard The Horseman and turned the lantern off and you took off running. So, my question is what did you see and what were you saying?"

"Shadow? I thought it was you. Are you sure you didn't ask me anything before you turned the lantern off?"

"No. it wasn't me, I think both, the Shadow and The Horseman were ghosts. Now that I think about it, it gives me the creeps!"

"I thought you said you were not afraid of ghosts." I said clasping my canteen belt.

"Okay, I lied, but don't you ever tell anybody or else." He said, as we picked up our backpacks and started down the trail.

Through the clearing of tall tree tops we could get a glimpse of the winding trail far down the slopes and farming fields. Beyond that, the trail would branch, and I would be home after three more hours of hiking. The right fork would take Victor on a more gentle terrain a couple hours to Valle Verde his home town.

"Else what?"

"I won't tell you about this other mysterious place…"

"What place?

"There is this ancient Church with a tunnel hidden under the steps… legend has it that the entire church was built in one single night by the devil himself and…"

"Yeah, yeah." I cut him short. "And I am sure there is a treasure as well, and nobody else dares to go, right? But you know what? Ask somebody else. I am going to be extremely busy... being a poor farmer."

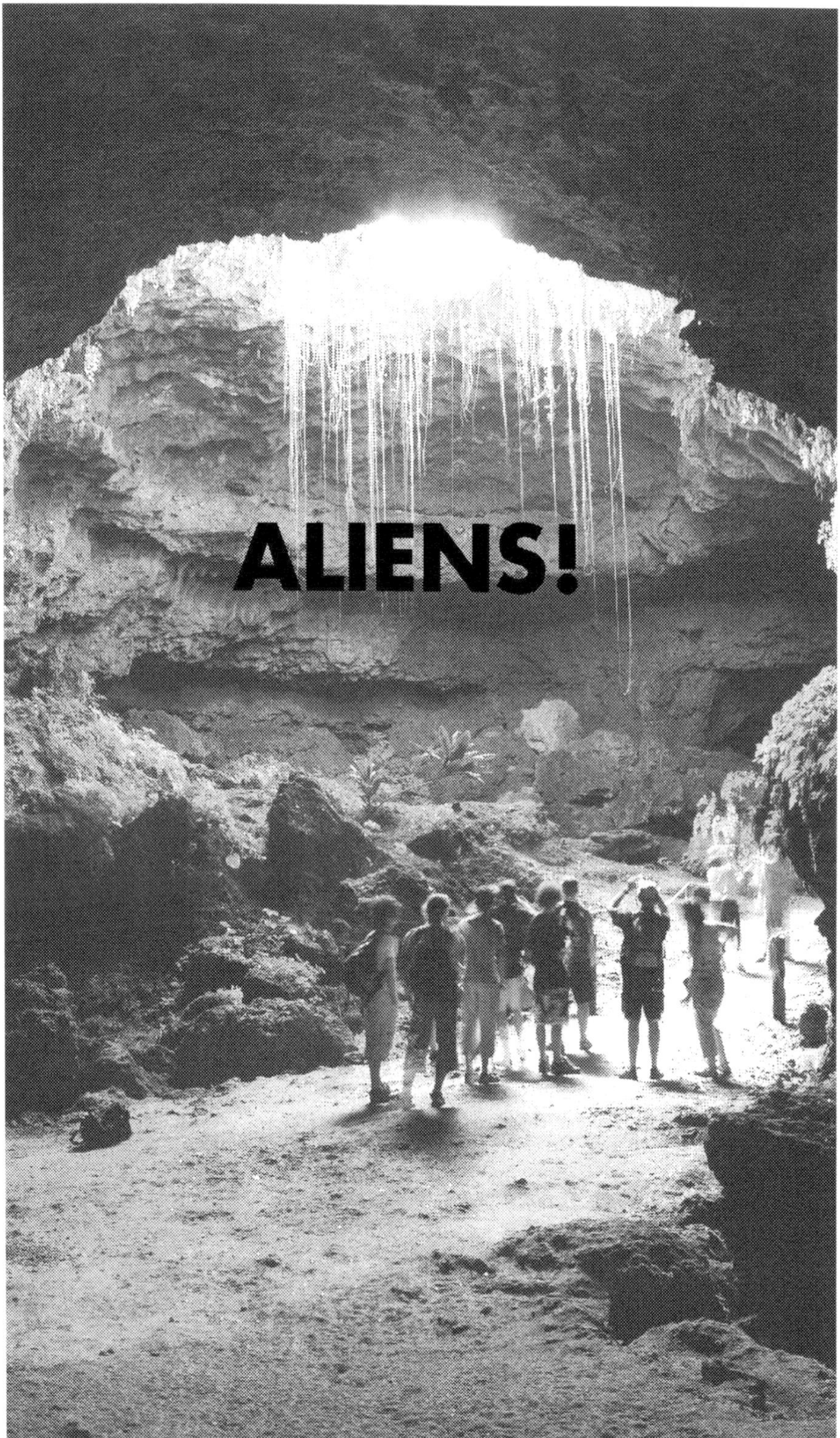
ALIENS!

The spaceship had crashed on a desolated and rocky terrain. Now it was pitch dark and at this distance it was hard to tell how big it was because only part of it stuck out of the ground. As I got closer I could see that the visible part rose up some fifty feet up in the air and flames and smoke came from within.

My vehicle approached fast and hard. It banked to the right to avoid grazing the debris surrounding the area. A sharp turn just ahead was too much for my vehicle that started to spin out of control. Onboard computers immediately switched to master control. Anti-collision systems kicked in and reversing thrusters dissipated the kinetic energy into a wide turn. Out of nowhere, a spider-like alien rose from the ground swinging a massive ray gun. I rolled my laser weapon and squeezed the trigger. The alien emitted a painful shriek and dropped to the ground.

Red pencils of light searched for my ship trying to lock and destroy the intruder. The crew of my ship was missing; I dashed left and right spraying death to rematerializing creatures. I had to get out of Dodge and fast. I zigzagged out at supersonic speeds from the deadly ambush under heavy fire and came to a clear.

The display on my dashboard read 999,999 points and it was flashing.

"Congratulations, Earthling." The computer-generated voice came on the speakers. "You have reached a perfect score."

I keyed in the mic attached to my breast pocket. "Tech-five to Control Tower, all Aliens are operational; Audio checks good, FX good, weapons check, vehicles check and video is O.K."

The vehicle spun 360 degrees again and rolled to the unload area before coming to a smooth stop.

"Ten four, Tech five, good job out there," the reply came from the control tower.

The all eyes in the sky monitoring system maintained a constant watch and surveillance on one of the most modern and advanced rides of a thematic amusement parks in the world. Here, just for this particular ride alone, more than 200 computers worked in concert to immerse visitors into a life-like experience with Aliens and not necessarily of the illegal kind.

Having worked for this amusement park for a number of years I had been involved in projects ranging from programming animatronics, building robotic figures, troubleshooting hydraulics and pneumatics, test flight simulators, design special effects (FX) such as, flame and fire explosions, water explosions, fog effects, creating all kinds of electrical and electronic devices, assisting stunt actors in shooting commercials or TV series to working with cryogenics equipment and assisting the scuba diving team for underwater repair.

Although now I was working in the make-believe world of entertainment, my interest in the real extraterrestrial life forms, had begun early in childhood, when I would listen to the radio shows or read the hard-to-get magazines of science fiction. But most intriguing of all was watching those strange lights on the cliff of the mountain darting to the higher peaks, hang in there for a little bit, then disappear.

My mother believed that they were witches and that the only way to catch them was saying Psalm 23 backwards, which she promptly would set to do, helped by my two older sisters. Of course, by the time they got two or three words out, it was just chaos and the witches, meanwhile, were on their merry way out of sight.

Why she wanted to catch them is beyond me, but according to legend, if you followed the precise instructions, the witch would appear nearby tied up in a neat bundle. Undeterred, my mother and sisters would run inside, dig the Bible out, and then read Psalm 23 backwards. I was; meanwhile, busy barricading myself behind a window, armed with a long stick and peeking outside looking for suspicious bundles.

The village was perched high above on the slopes of the Sierra Madre, the long mountain chain that runs along central Mexico. The region, forbidden to most visitors due to its impregnable natural barriers of steep slopes, thick jungle, deep canyons and torrential rains, had been for centuries, the unspoiled sanctuary for an almost extinct group of Indians known as The Huastecos.

The Huastecos did not have a proper village but lived scattered across the mountains with coffee and banana plantations surrounding each hut. Foot trails under the dense canopy connected to other huts beyond the hills.

By the mid-fifties, when I was born, I am tempted to say that Villa Vincenzo was a sleepy village, but it wasn't. It was more like the Old West. A main trail cut through the town and waved its way up and down the lesser hills along the skirt of the long mountain range that extends beyond the horizon in both directions. The town spread out under the shadow of the mountain that rose hundreds of feet up into the sky. High cliffs faced the town but large parts of them were covered by thick green vegetation. To the east, the slope of the mountain just continued down, with a magnificent view of the mountains far below that extended to the purple horizon as far as the eye could see.

The trail along the mountain connected other towns about an hour walk apart. None of these towns had electricity, phone, running water or medical services. The nearest town that had a road was five hours away down the main trail where packs of mules were used to carry goods to and from. The trail was extremely hard to traverse; it was narrow and in many places just wide enough for one way traffic and precipices of shear straight drops with fog over the tree tops below. The rains made it extremely hard to negotiate, where the mules would sink in the mud to their bellies and the heavy loads imposed on them were murderous and inhuman.

Whenever one of the locals developed an illness, there was no place nearby to go or get medical treatment. Children would die of high fever or from a snake bite, a cut or a fall was just as deadly.

Why had these people chosen to live in such an inhospitable place? According to several accounts, early in the nineteenth century, people left towns and cities to find refuge in the mountains from the civil wars. In their minds the farther away from civilization the better, they would live off the land and in harmony with nature.

Those had been my grandparents and at that time they may have been justified. But my parents, who had gone through all this suffering, were still willing to continue the pattern because of the "this-is-our-land" credo.

My father had a small general store in the outskirts of town and my vivid memories as a child are of the cow herd drives going through town. Hundreds of cows and ferocious bulls stampeding down the trail, the point cowboy in front of the herd calling with a "toooo, toooo" would disappear in the distance in a cloud of dust but the long procession would still be going strong in front of our house. More cowboys flanked the herd and some more pushed the rear whistling and yelling encouraging the herd or sprinting on their fast horses to regroup and round up the strays. Their lassoes would smoke on the horns of the saddle when reining in the reluctant beasts. The tinkling spurs on the cowboys boots was the familiar sound on the cobblestoned front of the store where after a few beers and shots of Rum they would go on their way.

We lived near a cemetery that was just up the hill. It was lined with ancient maple trees. A water spring was just past the cemetery where my mom had to go to get water one bucket at time. There was another house beyond the water spring. Amidst banana trees and orange groves stood a dilapidated hut, its walls, made out of sticks tied with the flexible bark of a tree were so thin that you could see not just the interior but through and across the other side. The roof made out of palm leaves was no better. Deep holes on the dirt floor marked the downpours.

There, lived an old woman in raggedy clothes and white hair that seemed to be blowing in the wind all the time. She lived by herself surrounded by cats and dogs. What was unusual and terrifying about her was a white and bulging eye that moved in the opposite direction as the other one. Most of her teeth were missing except for two on the front that were yellowish, blackened and crooked.

As a young child my two older sisters would take me on their wanderings looking for wild berries and flowers into the woods, often times we ended up near the old woman's house. She would come out yelling and screaming at us and then would let loose the dogs from hell. I remember my sisters stampeding downhill still clutching the berries on their aprons and dragging me like a rag doll through the thorny bushes, feeling on my butt every single stump and rock down the hill all the way home.

"Why is the baby bleeding to death?" My mom would ask my sisters. "The baby? We have no idea, but look, we have some delicious berries. You want some?"

One day down the trail came a little dog; it stopped there on the other side of the trail as if afraid to get close to the house. It was drenched in sweat and thick crusts of mud hung from its belly. "The owner will show up soon." My mom said. "But give it some water." After it emptied the little bowl, it followed me into the house.

No one ever showed up to claim it.

We called him Solovino, the Spanish for "came by itself." Solovino would keep my mom company when my father, not busy going to town for supplies, would go tend the small patches of coffee plantations scattered throughout the mountain downrange.

My mom, years later, related to us an incident. One day when my dad was away and we were still little; it was close to midnight, when she heard knocking on the door. It was unusual for travelers to venture on long treks at night from distant towns. But that night was clear. There was a full moon and one could see in the open far in the distance. This gave you a false sense of relief, because under the trees that lined the trail was even darker than a wolf's mouth.

"Who is it?" My mom asked somewhat puzzled. Usually, Solovino would start barking way before anyone approached the house. This time, however he hadn't. He retreated, growling, tail between its hind legs, but without averting its eyes from the door.

"Who is it?" My mom asked again.

No response.

Often times when strangers came to the house, they would greet politely and ask for the man or woman of the house.

My mom reached for the machete hanging on the wall. Turned the kerosene lamp off and waited there by the bed where we were sleeping. The red glow from the coals in the clay stove cast a glow on Solovino there lying on the dirt floor. A gust of wind blew and rattled the loose wooden shingles on the roof.

From the corral on the other side of the house the mules started neighing and whimpering, terrified by someone or something. Solovino was still growling but this time its eyes and ears were pointing in the corral direction. A horse had been tied up with a long rope to graze on the other side of the trail, just a stone throw away from the cemetery. Now it was the horse's turn, Solovino's eyes and ears still tracking the sounds. After a long nerve wrecking time the neighing stopped and Solovino got up like nothing had ever happened.

Early in the morning, the following day, my mom went to check on the horse. There was nothing unusual, but when she tried to take it to the water spring past the cemetery the horse refused, rearing and bucking, to go anywhere near the cemetery. The horse pointed his ears and terrified eyes as if something was still there. She did not notice anything out of the ordinary in or around the cemetery then or afterwards but, since then, Solovino, just like the horse, refused to go to the water spring or near the cemetery.

I must have been around five years old, when we moved to another house closer to the center of town. A new school was being built next to the town church. I was relieved and happy to move away from the cemetery.

The old owners of our new house had left, among other things, an old wooden crib. It had its handrails carved with mysterious signs and inscriptions. The crib was big enough for me, but it was my little brother, now two years old, the one who would sleep there. About two weeks later, my little brother started talking in his sleep, and then he would wake up and start crying for no reason. Soon, he started getting up in his sleep, go outside come back to bed and keep snoring like nothing ever happened. My mom would gather a bunch of herbs and sweep my little brother up and down to banish and cleanse the bad spirits.

When that didn't work, he was taken to a bed next to my mom so she could keep an eye on his nocturnal wanderings. I was then, to my delighted surprise, allowed to sleep in the crib.

Soon the nightmares started.

I remember one in particular. I was lost in the forest near a lake with dark water. It was dense with fog with nightfall approaching; the bushes and rocks were coming to life and started to morph into gigantic black snakes. I cried for help but barely a whisper came out, I tried to run and my feet sank in the swamp. So vivid and terrifying was the nightmare's grip that I was unable to wake up even though my mom was shaking me and frantically calling me to wake up. My mom says that I was crying and my eyes were wide open. I remember hearing her soothing voice. "I'm here honey don't be afraid. It's me, Mom." In my dream I desperately looked around only to see the voice coming from an even more horrifying snake.

After repeated episodes, I was still refusing to relinquish the crib, but every night I would fear falling asleep, I would fight to stay awake knowing the nightmare would be there as soon as I closed my eyes. When I started getting sick and even more powerful herbs failed to banish the stubborn bad spirits, my mother realized it was the crib. My father promptly destroyed it and used it as firewood. Afterwards the nightmares stopped and my little brother never sleepwalked again. Years later we learned that a little girl had died in that crib; was it cursed? And what about those strange carved inscriptions?

We may never know.

When I was six years old I started going to the recently built makeshift school. It had a roof made out of palm leaves, no walls and a floor made out of compressed dirt. A local man that knew little how to read and a lot less how to write was volunteering to teach us, a handful of raggedy and barefooted kids, the alphabet and basic arithmetic.

During the summer he took us on a field trip, about three miles away, to The Sotano de las Golondrinas, The Cave of Swallows. This was a huge crater in the middle of the jungle. Cut through solid rock, a black bottomless pit around 1,400 feet deep and some 200 feet in diameter. There, inside lived millions of swallows, bats and colorful parakeets. In the morning they would come out from the depths circling the walls of the cave like a whirlwind and the noise generated and amplified by the cave resembled that of a water fall. A black tornado of birds would climb up high and disappear beyond the jungle. In the evening they would return and a huge black cloud would form high up in the sky above the cave. Suddenly the cloud would crumble and in a choreographed move, the center of the cloud would pour straight down from hundreds of feet up in the sky and dive into the cave in an amazing display of sight and sound.

The shape of this geological wonder did not resemble an extinct volcano, nor did it have the typical shape of a meteorite crater. The mouth or opening was even smaller than the interior in a concave or bell shape fashion. Early American expeditions in the late 1960's discovered a river in its deep interior at the end of a long tunnel. To my knowledge more recent expeditions have failed to uncover the cave origins.

Further away, some three hours on foot and several mountains away, another unusual event took place. A valley, known by the locals as "Las Joyas" or lowlands, were depressions and valleys surrounded by higher mountains. During the rainy season, whenever it rained for more than four straight days, these valleys became lakes. These valleys were not small; they ran some eight miles wide and lengthwise extended as far as the eye could see, when flooded, distant hills barely crested over the water level.

The main trail to civilization was cut for several days. What is truly amazing is the speed at which the water appeared and disappeared. It would be completely dry and three hours later completely flooded. No logical explanation has ever been found.

Not long ago a friend of mine, Jorge Cruz that lives in Mexico, invited me to join him on an expedition to another strange and mysterious place. He gave me just enough information and hints to pique my curiosity.

"I want you to see it for yourself" He said, knowing my affinity for the unknown.

He met me at the bus station of a small town in the Northern part of Mexico. From there we drove to his house and spent the night swapping stories by the campfire. The following day we drove for several hours through thick vegetation and dirt roads. We crisscrossed several shallow rivers in his all-terrain and off-road vehicle.

The dirt road ended by a small village. The quilt of tin roofs with streaks of rust shone under the tropical sun, contrasting with those of black tar scattered at the base of the hill. There we were joined by two local men that greeted us in a very friendly manner.

"We are ready to take you to The Place" The older one said.

"You don't even need to carry any water, there is plenty where we're going." The younger one added.

Still, I got my canteen and strapped it on my backpack just in case, my friend did the same and off we went.

"First we're going to see the river." my friend said pointing up a trail into the woods.

The two men in front were clearing and chopping the occasional fallen branches with their machetes until we got to an opening. There from a cave, at the base of the hill, the river gushed out.

"That." Said Jorge pointing to the river, "is the only river that we kept crossing."

"It makes you wonder where it is coming from." I said over the noise.

Jorge pointed up hill. "You'll see it."

The two local guides were already heading up the steep trail with the confidence and dexterity of those who have done it countless times. By the time Jorge and I managed to reach the crest of the hill, they were waiting for us sitting there on big boulders and smiling.

The top of the hill was semi-flat, but trees and bushes didn't let you see very far. We walked to the edge of the mesa where you could see down below on the other side of the hill. There it was. A huge perfectly circular crater some two hundred feet in diameter cut from solid rock and filled with water. The water level stood some thirty feet below the rim's edge. On the water, several small islands covered with tall grass moved slowly. It was an impressive sight.

"What does it remind you of?" Jorge said with a puzzling face.

"El Sotano de las Golondrinas" I said without thinking twice.

"Exactly." my friend said. "Except that this is filled with water."

"What's that on the far edge... it looks like a..." I was squinting my eyes.

"Yeah, it is a cross to mark the spot where a few years back a member of an American deep sea diving team died."

"What were they doing here?"

"Nobody knows for sure. Some say they were just sport cave diving, others think they were a group of NASA scientists with a secret agenda. But if they were, what were they looking for?" Jorge paced back and forth.

"Did he run out of oxygen?" I pointed to the cross.

"No, the ones that survived say that they were several hundred feet down when the team leader in front got caught in a maelstrom, a very strong and turbulent current, and they just saw him disappear, his lights just spinning into darkness." The two local guides nodded.

"Yes, I was with them," said the older one.

"We were sent to look downstream" he said pointing to the other side of the hill. "We searched the river for two days, but we didn't find anything." The other one added.

"On the third day," Jorge retook the narrative, "the body resurfaced, right where the cross is."

"He still had the oxygen tanks strapped to his body." piped in the younger of the guides.

"Totally empty" Jorge added.

This was indeed very strange, and what a terrible way to die. I could almost feel the struggle, the desperation, the pressure...

"So what did they do afterwards?" I was curious.

"Nothing, they just took their dead friend and left."

"Did anybody return afterwards? Other teams?"

"No." the two men shook their heads.

"You want to see the other ones?" The younger of the two men pointed to the circular lake.

"You mean there are more like this?"

"Not quite like this one." Jorge said. "They are smaller."

We went down the hill past the large Cenote.

"Hey! Maybe that's what it is" I told Jorge. "In the Yucatan peninsula the Mayas offered human sacrifices to the Gods by throwing young virgins into the sacred "Cenotes", which were bottomless water pits."

"It is possible" Jorge said "Maybe the divers were trying to find out if there is any connection between them, and the river."

About a quarter mile down we came to a small water pond, also circular, a lot smaller, maybe some eighty feet in diameter. But in this one you could see the shallow bottom. Farther down at the base of the hill, just before a long stretch of flat terrain with corn fields, there was another circular area about one hundred and fifty feet in diameter. But unlike the other ones, only a small section had water, you could actually walk and see the far edge of the circle under trees and vegetation.

"Let's go take a look at the cave" Jorge nodded to the men.

In front of us lay a large flat terrain.

"Are we heading in the right direction?" I said looking at the hills in the back.

"You just keep going." They were smiling.

The sun was now high up in the sky blasting down merciless and the trees were far in between to be of any assist with the shade. But that was not all, red signs on the side of the path read "Private Property, No Trespassing".

"Don't worry about it" Jorge said. "The armed goons that patrol it are not always here."

We walked for a little while when, without a warning, the trail ramped down into a hidden depression not seen from afar and into a cave entrance under the flat terrain. Entering the cave I could see a tunnel to the right and a tunnel to the left. The one on the right side extended for a short distance ending abruptly, blocked by huge boulders.

The one on the left continued on and as we walked I noticed that we were not using our flashlights. At set intervals, there were circular openings on the cave's roof where natural light just poured in. As the light from one source started to fade there would be another one that took over and the pattern continued deep down the winding length to a huge chamber with cathedral-like walls. Just beyond the cathedral the tunnel was blocked, again, by huge boulders the size of a car.

Those huge stones did not appear to be part of the cave itself. Someone or something had put them there and they appeared to be blocking or hiding something. The wall and roof gave all appearances that the tunnel continued farther down.

I retraced my steps to take a closer look to those roof openings. They were angled right to where the light was needed. My observation from where I was standing indicated a smooth cut of several feet off the solid rock.

"These openings do not look natural." I said to my companions.

"So, you think they're man-made" Jorge said skeptically.

"No," I said still wondering at my own thoughts. "They are Alien-made."

"What?" he was taken aback by my assertion, but so was I.

"You must be kidding, right?" he repeated, but my brain was in overdrive now.

"The ponds! They are spaceships that crash-landed some Millennia in the past. Alien survivors built these caves to live in and the roof openings were made by some type of laser guns!"

"Next thing you're going to say is that maybe they're still here, huh?"

"Not bad, you're a fast learner."

"What's your theory?"

"I think the cave diver got too close to discover something, or who knows, maybe he did and he had to be eliminated to keep the secret." I realized this sounded like the script of a bad movie.

"Maybe the diving team was indeed a group of scientists that were investigating UFOs." Jorge was thinking hard.

"Do you know if they came to the cave?"

Jorge didn't know. He bounced the question to the older man.

"No, I don't think so." He said.

"Have you seen anything unusual around this area? Like lights..."

"UFOs, have you seen any?" Jorge cut in.

The old man didn't say anything but the young one hesitated for a little bit. "No." he finally said. "But sometimes we hear a noise coming from this area." Maybe we were onto something.

"What kind of noise?"

"Like that of a hurricane, like strong wind..."

Out of the corner of my eye I caught a glimpse of the old man exchanging a kind of signal with the young one, but thought nothing of it.

"When you hear this noise, do you feel the wind? Or see the trees bending..."

"No."

"And you haven't seen anything."

"No."

"We have to go." Jorge said looking at his watch "It is getting late."

We did continue the discussion until the following day when I had to return to The States. We made plans to one day organize an expedition to explore and study the cave more in depth and, who knows, maybe uncover the find of the century.

It wasn't until my airplane was cruising at 35,000 feet on my way home that the nagging feeling I had during our conversation in the cave returned.

Now I knew what it was.

The two local guides; their eyes were big, black and their heads unusually large.

Rio Bravo

It was a narrow clearing through the tall grass, loose dirt and gravel turned to sandy soil that ramped down to shallow water on the Mexican side. It was pitch dark. The two women were barefoot and each one carried their belongings in a small plastic bag. The kid had stripped down to his underwear and was shivering in the midnight cold. The Coyote in front stopped the single file and, in hushed tones, ordered the three to lie down. On the other side of the river a vehicle was moving slowly away, its lights turned off, but the red glow of its brake lights gave it away.

"Was that La Migra?" whispered one of the women.

The Coyote didn't answer, instead, he said. "Quick! We have only twenty minutes to make it to the other side before immigration comes back," and pushed two inflated inner tubes into the water.

"Estela dile al coyote que yo no sé nadar." There was panic and fear in the woman's voice.

"Don't worry if you don't know how to swim." The reassuring voice said next to her. "Get inside the inner tube, you too kid, hold on tight and we're going to push you, and keep your voice down for God's sake!"

Slowly they eased into the dark waters holding each other at arm's length.

Sharp rocks and debris littered the bottom forcing the group to a slow crawl. By now their eyes had grown accustomed to the dark and could see each other's shapes. For a short distance water level was steady chest high, suddenly the bottom gave way. Desperate splashing and muffled cries pierced the night. Only then, the Coyote turned his water proof flashlight on. The makeshift lifesaver where the older lady was a second ago was empty and heavy bursts of bubbles were moving downstream.

"Son of a bitch!" he cursed as he unclipped his hand from the rope that held the tubes together. "Keep going" he said to the young lady and dove into the dark waters. Now mother and son found themselves alone, she was swimming hard to fight the current.

"Mama tengo miedo!" her son had started to cry.

"I'm here son, we'll make it." All she had to do was to stay focused on that red light flashing on a steel tower far in the distance.

After what seemed like a long time she felt the sandy bottom, there was movement straight ahead. Mother and son were briefly in the center of a flashlight beam, but no loudspeakers or men in green uniforms.

"It's me" the Coyote said in a whisper, but he was alone.

"Oh God! Where is Rosa?" she cried.

The Rio Grande, better known to the locals as The Rio Bravo, separates the sister cities; McAllen on the American side and Reynosa on the Mexican side just across the international bridge. Countless have died in its waters, swept by the deceptive current. Bodies have been recovered many miles downstream and their unclaimed corpses lay in the morgue for a long time.

"Relax!" he started towing the kid. "She's on the other side."

When they reached the other side Rosa was lying on her knees still coughing water and shaking.

"Estela! Santo Dios. I thought I'd never see you again!" They hugged.

"Vamos! Rapido!" The Coyote was letting the air out of the tubes. They climbed up the loose dirt, and ran through the sharp blades of the tall grass and thorny bushes. A short distance from the river they came to a clearing and a dirt road where an all-terrain vehicle was waiting in the dark. The Coyote threw his gear in the trunk, ushered the trio in the rear seats and motioned to the female driver.

"Go! Go! Go!" loose dirt flew as the car peeled off.

Once they were on the main road they mingled with the light traffic. Careful to avoid unnecessary attention, aware that often times, minor traffic violations were the downfall of major operations. The Coyote opened the glove compartment and pulled out a cell phone, punched a number and said, "We're clear."

Ten miles up north in a quiet neighborhood in the outskirts of Phar, Texas, a second female driver acknowledged the message. It was twenty five minutes past midnight, and the second phase of the mission was set in motion. The four door sedan gained access to Route 281 and headed south for the International Bridge.

The neon sign outside the restaurant read "El Paraiso." Perhaps, in its halcyon days, it had been a paradise. But times had changed and the once quiet neighborhood was now a hive of activity. Again, El Paraiso Restaurant had been chosen for the rendezvous not for its food or service, let alone for the company of seedy characters at the next table. The ambience reminded me of "La Cantina" from Star Wars. A hazy cloud hung in the air and a whiff of stale beer drifted from the bar. I did a quick, yet discrete, scan to the dim lit surroundings. No, no Bounty Hunters today. El Paraiso was conveniently located, for this and other shady dealings, just a few blocks away from the International Bridge.

I had carefully selected the table at the opposite entrance wall and off to the side so that I could keep an eye on any new customer that drifted in. I looked at my watch; it was fifty five minutes past midnight. If everything had gone as planned my sister Estela, nephew Christian and Cousin Rosa, should be on the other side. The two year old kid seated with me, younger nephew Mickey, at the table started to cry again. From my duffel bag I pulled a candy bag with the last marshmallow. He stopped crying.

"Look" I was going to cut it, "I'm going to give you a piece..." He screamed.

"All right, all right, take it all." This was going to buy me another two minutes at most. I made a mental note, "next time, buy hard candy."

I had ordered a meal, then dessert, but that was ages ago and the little kid was growing restless. I feared the worst. What if they got caught? The lady was supposed to meet me here forty minutes ago. Now I had been seated at the table for almost two hours and it was beginning to seem odd at best. Not that the patrons cared one way or the other, I was ready to bet that if Jack the Ripper strode in with a corpse in tow, hardly anybody would've given him a second look. But...I was with a baby and I was getting second looks from the waiter.

Two women in high heels and low cut dresses strolled in by my table and squeezed the baby's cheeks "Hi! Sweetie! Would you like a good time?" one said.

"I'm sorry," I said "I don't think he..."

"I was talking to you." She giggled and walked away.

Out of the corner of my eye I noticed the waiter talking to an older man, he had been taking orders from, darting suspicious looks in my direction.

The manager then grabbed the phone from the wall and dialed a number. He said something and again he gazed at my table. I had to get out of Dodge and fast.

My beeper buzzed. And the kid started crying.

A woman dressed in black and a white scarf flowing in the wind stood hesitant by the entrance. In a swift motion I swept the kid and my bag and bolted for the door.

The manager turned. "Hey you!" the phone left dangling from the cord.

The woman in black and white scarf grabbed my bag as we sprinted down the street. She pointed to a brown sedan parked in a dark alley. We got in and zigzagged out of the narrow streets and before I realized we were approaching the Mexican checkpoint.

Only one of several gates had the green light and two vehicles were in front of us. With only a cursory inspection of front and rear seats, the first car was waved away. The second car, a blue Firebird-Trans-Am with T-tops, Mag wheels and New York license plates went through a more detailed inspection and then was ordered to move to the side. The officer approached our car; he peeked in the rear seat where the kid was now surprisingly quiet in the baby seat. He briefly glanced at the local green card held by the woman at the wheel. I was holding my passport in front of me, but he wasn't interested he waved us through.

"Wow, we made it!" I said with relief.

"Not yet," she pointed to the American side.

There were no other cars at the checkpoint. We stopped at the gate blocked by a black and yellow striped cross-barrier. The officer in the tan uniform double checked her facial features against her ID. Once he was satisfied, he turned to me, and noticed the kid in the back seat.

"Are you two married?" he said, scrutinizing my passport, but looking at her.

"No, he's my cousin here for a visit" she casually answered.

He looked at me again and said. "What do you do in Chicago?"

"I work for a Corporation that manufactures video equipment and..."

"That's good." he cut in.

"I want you to step outside of the car Ma'am." He said to the woman, he pointed at me, "You stay where you are."

He ordered the woman to open the trunk. He did a brisk inspection and after he was satisfied he returned her ID and my passport. The kid had started to cry.

"What's up with the kid?" he inquired.

"My son's been sick and I took it to the Curandera, you know."

"Oh I see" he said with a smile, how was it possible that this Mexican still believed in Witch doctors? Well, that was not his problem.

"Have a good night." He waved us through.

We were a good distance away when I finally let out a sigh of relief. "For a minute I thought he was going to ask us for the kid's documents."

She just smiled and tapped the glove compartment. "My son is about the same age." She then speed dialed a number and said. "We're clear."

I was glad I was working with pros.

When we arrived at the house, Rosa and Estela were still shaken and wrapped in towels. The kid with me ran to hug his mom, Estela was crying. The Coyote was drinking a beer in front of the TV; he pulled another one from the fridge and motioned for me to follow outside.

"Everything came out all right." he said.

"Thanks, I really like the way you did it." I handed him a stash of bills. "This is the balance and we want to leave first thing in the morning."

"Let's get some sleep now; we'll talk about it tomorrow."

The following day, The Coyote's wife took my sister and cousin to shop for clothes and shoes since they had lost everything in the river.

I stayed home with The Coyote.

"By bus from here to Houston it's still risky." He took a long draw from his beer. "There are quite a few checkpoints along the way. Right off the bat is Falfurrias on 281 and that's a tough one."

"So what do you suggest?"

"There is a couple other ways, but it's more complicated." He pushed another beer my way and popped open another one for himself. "If you can," he continued, "buy plane tickets for tomorrow, which is Sunday." He looked me in the eye. "Not noon, not in the evening, it has to be Sunday morning."

"Why is that so?"

"It is the only time when you can board a plane without being scrutinized." I was all ears. He told me about other methods and tricks he had used in the past and why some didn't work anymore.

Later that day we went to buy the plane tickets. "Pay with credit Card." he said. "That way you don't need to present their ID's."

He did other freelance jobs.

Without being specific, he related a time when he had taken three Colombians across the border and all the way to Louisiana. He had agreed in part, because they were not carrying any bags or luggage; plus, the initial large payment and the promise of more at the final destination was very tempting. After traveling most of the night they crossed into Louisiana, they asked him to detour around Lake Charles. They were going to pick up something and then continue to the next town. They arrived at a secluded and gated mansion. Inside a pack of vicious Dobermans patrolled the grounds. "I'm not going in there." He told them. "I'll wait for you outside."

He was dozing off when several shots rang inside. In his rearview mirror he saw one of the Colombians running to the gate, with the Dobermans in hot pursuit, and just behind, a guy in pajamas wielding a gun. The Colombian was only steps from the gate when more shots rang out and, his bloody hands clawing on the gate, slipped to the floor.

"I floored the gas all the way home." He said of his close call.

Of course he didn't know what kind of business they were involved in. I wasn't interested either.

He excused himself he said he had to go do a job and that we would not see each other again.

"Anything you need." He said before he left. "My wife and sister can handle it."

Now all we had to do was; wait for Sunday morning.

We were almost there, but I couldn't let my guard down, not yet. This was a roller coaster and I was getting more than I had bargained for. Three weeks ago in Chicago my plan was simple. All I wanted to do was to visit my Mom in Mexico. I had planned to spend two relaxed weeks by the beach sipping colored drinks with little umbrellas. But things had turned out a little different.

At my mom's house it had been nothing but celebration the first days. She had been busy cooking the spicy enchiladas she was famous for. But you had to taste the gorditas con queso y guacamole. You couldn't really ask for more.

But her eyes betrayed sadness. The following day I found her crying, and she wouldn't tell me. Finally she said. "It's Estela."

"Estela? What's up with her?" My sister and her two kids lived in Mexico City.

"The man she lives with is extremely abusive to her."

"Why is she staying? Can't she just leave him?"

"She did. She went to stay with a lady friend, hoping he would not find her. Two weeks later he did and dragged her back to his apartment, beat her up and told her that if she tries that one more time he's going to kill her." Her eyes swelled with tears. "I'm really worried about her."

"Can she get a restraining order?"

"It would not work, and it will just make him angrier." I wasn't surprised, Mexico being one of the leading countries where more women die as a result of domestic violence.

"Is she working?"

"Not anymore. Carlos, that's the guy's name, does not allow her to go out, period."

"Bastard! I'm going to go and teach the son of a bitch a lesson!"

"No please, now you see, that's why I didn't want to tell you anything."

"Can she come over and stay with you?"

"She could. But this was the first place he checked last time."

"Maybe she and the kids can go elsewhere, but where?"

"I was talking to your Aunt Vicky the other day and she said they can go live with her but..."

"Tia Vicky. In Houston, Texas?"

"Yes, but..."

"Mom that could be the ideal solution, yes I know what you're thinking... they can't get a visa." We knew this from personal experience. You can't expect to apply for a visa and obtain one. First there is the incredible amount of documents you have to present. Then there is the lengthy wait period that can go from months to years. In the end you are just told that you do not qualify because you need tens of thousands of dollars in your bank account. It is like trying to get a loan from a Bank, you have to prove that you DON'T need one to qualify.

There was only one way and I had only one week to do it.

Aging buses made the one way trip from Tampico to Mexico City in twelve hours on winding roads hanging from the cliffs across the Sierra Madre through the States of Veracruz, Hidalgo and Estado de Mexico.

When I arrived to Mexico City the following day, it was still dark and first light was a good hour away, but the city was already bustling with life. Vendors, buses, delivery trucks and the beetle taxi cabs trying to outdo each other in cramming the most passengers. The air was crisp and the scent of coffee and food came from the Taquerias nearby selling atole, tacos de carnitas, al pastor, and adobada.

I was traveling light, only a small back pack with one extra change of clothes, and a light jacket. I boarded "El Metro", the high speed transportation network, at the "Indios Verdes" station. Throngs of people were rushing to fill the already overloaded cars. At some connecting stations females were separated and assigned exclusive cars in an attempt to maintain some order. The struggle was on, passengers had to fight to stay in or get out. In the crowded melee a teenager was tugging at my backpack, I turned and sank my elbow into his ribs, with a muffled yelp he sank to the floor and disappeared from sight. Nobody seemed to care or notice. Welcome to Mexico City.

I exited the last train station and when I showed the note with the hand written address at the newspaper stand the old man said. "Esa direccion queda por la Barranca del Muerto y para alla no van buses."

"Como puedo llegar?"

"Aqui a la vuelta hay taxis."

La Barranca Del Muerto, The Dead Man's Creek, was a far flung rundown neighborhood at the edge of the city surrounded by "ciudades perdidas", lost cities, a far resemblance of the ghettos from New York or the favelas from Rio. The courtyard was surrounded by a two story building, bare footed children played soccer on the dusty dirt floor while an overweight lady washed clothes on a stone slab next to two 55 gallon barrels filling with water from a dripping faucet. A dog by the first apartment noticed my presence first alerting the dwellers. I started walking towards the lady when the dog went for my leg.

"Stop it Poncho!" A kid in a raggedy shirt and dirty face came running and patted the dog.

"Thanks kid, look I'm looking for la senora Estela, do you know her?" The kid looked at me up and down. "Why do you want to see my mom?"

Although still in her twenties, my sister looked a lot older, a dress that had seen too many washes sagged on her thin body and her eyes were sunken. She was surprised by my unexpected arrival but happy to see me.

"Carlos is out of town and he's going to be out for three days." She said referring to her boyfriend. "He works for a trucking Company."

"Then we have no time to waste." I explained the escape plan.

"I'm scared," she said. "What am I going to do with all my stuff?" her stuff consisted mainly of second hand furniture and a few kitchen utensils that had seen better days, but nonetheless acquired with great effort.

"Forget about it, it is your life we're talking about. Just get your important documents, three or four changes of cloths for each and let's get out of here!"

"He's going to kill me!"

"Don't worry, we won't be here."

It was easier said than done. The following morning she was still trying to sell some of her stuff and tying up loose ends. My nerves were at the breaking point.

"This evening the lady from seven is going to pay me money she owes me."

"What?" I was adamant to not stay one more minute. "What if he comes today?"

"No, he won't be here until tomorrow."

Now I was desperate. Luckily, a little after noon we had loaded two suitcases, and the two kids on a taxicab.

We had driven a short distance, when coming the opposite way; a beat up pickup truck zoomed by trailing a cloud of dust.

"Daddy!" the six year old boy said pointing to the retreating cloud.

"That's him!" my sister was stunned.

"Go straight to the bus station." I said to the driver.

"Don't you want to go to the Metro station?"

"No, change of plans and the faster you get there the more you'll get." I said waving a wad of bills in my hand.

He floored the gas pedal as we were sucked in the back seats and the tires squealed.

The game was on.

We got to the bus station where at the ticket window the attendant said. "If you run you can catch the bus leaving on Gate nine." We boarded the bus and traveled most of the night. By three o'clock in the morning on the following day we were in Tampico at my mom's house. We slept for a few hours, but I knew we had to keep going. During breakfast a lady in her mid-thirties came in for a visit.

"Don't you remember your cousin Rosa?" My mom said.

I didn't, but Estela did and soon both were involved in deep conversation.

"Did you know that I worked in McAllen five years ago? It was only for about a year because then my father died and I had to come back. But what a coincidence I'm ready to go again!" Rosa wanted to come with us.

"I hope this doesn't cause us more problems." I told Estela when Rosa left.

"I don't think so." Estela said. "She is paying her own expenses, plus she knows her way around the border."

"Okay." I shrugged. I wasn't too sure.

A few hours later we boarded the bus headed north for Reynosa, about ten hours drive to the border.

"Bienvenidos a Reynosa" the welcoming sign read on the side of the road.

Reynosa, like most border cities and towns along the Rio Grande, grew and flourished because of the trade of goods between the two countries. Visitors, traders and people from all walks of life and nationalities populate the city, some have stayed by choice but for many, this has been the end of an arduous and painful trek trying to cross to the land of dreams, to the land of plenty, only to find misery and despair and more often than not; death. The illegal trade of goods and humans turned the city into a lawless and crime ridden frontier, where the Cartels and the Federales shoot first and ask questions later.

Welcome to the Border.

"Room 219 on the second floor," the clerk at the hotel desk said, handing me the key with a worn and faded tag number.

The following day, my sister stayed at the hotel with my two little nephews and I accompanied Rosa who wanted to meet her contacts. The taxicab took us to the outskirts of the city through dirt roads to a row of dilapidated adobe houses. The sun was blasting down in all its fury and the thin metal roofs were shimmering.

"Carmen is at work, but she won't be long. Please come in, you can wait inside." An old woman with missing teeth said at the door.

The dirt floor was swept clean and a broom made out of dry weeds tied to a rustic pole rested against the wall. "Please have a seat." she said motioning Rosa to the only available folding chair and handed me an empty five gallon bucket. Seeing my hesitation she turned it upside down on the floor and showing her missing teeth pointed to the makeshift stool.

Then it hit me, it was an overpowering stench that turned up my stomach, it came in waves and it seemed to originate from behind the wooden wall. The old woman offered us something to drink which I politely declined and excused myself to wait outside. It didn't take long before I was sorry, inside it had been ONLY the stench.

Outside, it was stinky and boiling.

After what seemed like hours the lady called Carmen came in. She went to the side of the house and let a monstrous pig out from the next room. The black swine run to the end of the patio where it dove into a mud pit brimming with trash and excrement.

Finally Rosa came out and she seemed in a good mood.

"I got the Coyote's phone that can take us to the other side." She handed to me a yellow piece of paper with the name Juan scribbled next to a phone number and an area code of the American side.

I was a little suspicious but not surprised, the only thing I wanted at that moment was to get out of there before I passed out.

"Next time remind me to just look for one in the Yellow Pages." She just looked at me wide eyed.

That evening I called the number. "Yes, we are friends of Carmen." I said when he inquired.

"Where are you staying?" He asked. I told him, and he seemed to think for a moment.

"Why don't we meet in the Main Square so we can talk?"

"Where, at the Main Square?"

"There is a Bank, Bancomex, across the street. Next to a newsstand there is a bench, sit there and read a newspaper. Meet me there in one hour. I will be wearing a black shirt and a tan fedora and we will say we are friends of Carmen." Then he hung up.

It was already dark when I arrived at the Plaza or Main Square. It was well before the appointed time but I did not want to take any chances. I approached the bench, and even though the mercury lights illuminated the surrounding area, the bench was under the shadow of a tree that overhung to the side walk.

I was surprised to see a man there already. He appeared to be dozing off and he had a dark shirt and sombrero. It wasn't a fedora, but...

I sat at the end of the bench and after several minutes of fiddling with my newspaper; I decided I had to make my next move.

"I am a friend of Carmen" I said to the shadow.

The shadow got up and now under the lights I could see an old and overweight man in a brownish shirt.

"You know my wife?"

I got up. "Sorry. Wrong Carmen," I quickly retreated mingling with a group of passersby.

"Hey, you!" he was calling in the distance.

I gave a wide berth across the street, circled the block and ended at the opposite end of the plaza where a street magician was performing surrounded by a group of onlookers that seemed to be amused by his cheap tricks and bad jokes, while his young accomplices worked the unsuspecting crowd.

I hang around; from a safe distance, to kill time. Just before the appointed time I headed back to the rendezvous point.

There was nobody sitting on the bench and only a few people there by the newsstand. I casually approached the bench, sat down and opened my newspaper. I must have looked ridiculous because I could not even make out the pictures.

"Can you read in the dark?"

I looked up and a young man in a dark shirt and tan fedora was smiling at me.

"Hi, I'm Juan." he said extending his hand. "I'm a friend of Carmen."

"You're lucky." I shoot back. When I recounted my earlier mishap he couldn't stop laughing.

We discussed the crossing and he laid out a plan for the following day.

"Around eleven at night my wife and I will pick all of you up from Carmen's house. My wife will drop four of us, me, your sister Estela with son Christian, and Cousin Rosa at a point where I know we can cross the Rio Bravo. Mickey the little one, my sister can pass him as her own son, so you and Mickey will be dropped off, still on the Mexican side at a restaurant where you are going to wait until my group is safe on the other side. Only then my sister will come over to pick you up and, since you have your documents, the three of you will cross over the International Bridge."

"Why do I have to wait?" I said, failing to see the whole picture.

He took a deep draw at the cigarette. "Just in case, you never know." He said looking into the distance. He was right; no need to end up with the kid on the other side if they didn't make it.

"Well, how about if you don't make it?" I said thinking a backup plan or perhaps a plan B was on the pipeline.

"Don't worry. Everything is going to be all right."

Now I was.

"Okay, what about the money?" I said.

"It will be one thousand dollars, for all." He said nonchalant, as if he had been selling potatoes over the counter. "I will need half of it right now and the rest when we're on the other side."

He must have noticed my hesitation because he then said. "I'm only charging you this much because Carmen told me Rosa is her friend. But I normally charge twice as much."

I reached into my pocket, and he was already discretely scanning the surroundings. When it was clear I passed five bills under the newspaper. He put the bills in his pocket, and shook my hand. "Eleven PM at Carmen's" he had said before disappearing into the night.

Now three days later Sunday morning had arrived and we were headed for the airport.

"I hope we're not late." I said to the Coyote's wife.

"This is a local flight so you don't need the check-in-early time required for international flights. Plus you only have carry-on bags. This way you can arrive just in time to get to the plane. You don't want to linger in the waiting area too long and look suspicious."

She seemed to have been around the block quite a few times. She had helped Rosa, Estela and the kids to dress and look casual.

Now it was time for the big test.

A few people were lining up already at the check in counter. An airport security guard and an immigration official were casually scanning the crowd and letting them through the gate. I got the boarding passes and we headed for the airplane. Just as we left the counter the immigration officer stepped in front with his arm outstretched.

"Can I see your ID please?"

I pulled my American passport out and handed it to him. He took his time to do a cursory check while studying the crowd that was forming behind me.

"Are they with you?" He said pointing to Estela, Rosa and the two kids, who were very quiet.

"Yes, they're with me." I said with a poker face.

He handed back my passport. "You have a good trip, sir." and motioned us to the gate.

We arrived in Houston before noon. Aunt Vicky was waiting for us and happy to see us. I had a two hour stopover before continuing on to Chicago. We went to get something to eat at the food court and before I knew it, it was time for me to leave. I was relieved the ordeal was over and I knew they were safe and in good hands.

I made it to my apartment late in the evening. The landlady brought me a stack of mail from the previous two weeks.

"How was your vacation?" she inquired just out of formality.

"Same old, same old," she was already down the hallway; she wasn't interested in her tenants' affairs, and that suited me fine.

I had left my sister sufficient funds to last her a couple months, according to my calculations, that was enough to get her going while she found a job. That's why I was surprised when about three weeks later my phone rang and she was on the other end of the line.

"I hate to do this." she said. "But I need five hundred dollars." She sounded worried.

"Why?"

"Well, they're renting the apartment next door and I'd like to have my own space, you know. I'm going to babysit two kids, so I'm going to make enough for the rent. This is just for the deposit. I'll pay you back as soon as I can."

"Hey no problem, I think that's a good idea" The following day I wired the money and busy as I was with work and school thought nothing of it until a week later when Aunt Vicky called.

"I'm just calling to let you know that Estela is not here anymore." She said in a dreadful tone. "She left."

"Yes I know, she moved next door." I said.

"No, she didn't."

"No? Where did she go?"

"She went back to Mexico!"

"What?" I could not believe my ears. "That's impossible. Why would she do something like that?"

"I have no Idea. I tried to talk her out of it but she would not listen to me."

"When was this?"

"Yesterday, I tried to call you but you were not home."

"So do you think she's with my Mom now?"

"No, I hate to tell you this but soon after she arrived she was calling that boyfriend of hers in Mexico, and I don't know what he told her but he convinced her to go back with him."

"So this talk about renting an apartment. . ."

"Not true."

I was totally devastated I thought it could not get worse than going back to Mexico, but back to her abusive boyfriend was absolutely crazy. I felt betrayed, more than anything because she was the one that had called him. I vowed I would not talk to her for as long as I lived.

A few months later, my phone rang.

My mom was crying. "Estela died." She said between broken sobs on the other end of the international call.

"When, how?"

"I just received a call; they say it was from natural causes."

"Was she still living with that guy? Carlos or whatever his name was?"

"Yes."

My head was spinning with conflicting emotions. I didn't know what I felt. But of one thing I was certain.

No natural causes.

THE THIRTEENTH BULLET

The landlady's voice resonated down the gloomy and dark basement. The staccato of her high heels drifted down the stairway as the door closed behind two more figures following from her office and business at street level. It was rather unusual for her to visit this underground world, home of the semi-homeless, transients, or in my case poor college students. On those few occasions when she paid us a visit, it was mostly to let us know that the rent had just gone up, again, or to collect past due rent from procrastinating or forgetful tenants.

According to her archaic accounting methods you were past due a month in advance, even though you had the required advance month deposit and you were delinquent seconds past the hour. No grace period, period.

You either played by her rules or else.

Else was: Being evicted without the possibility of deposit return. The enforcer was a gorilla with a beer. His name was Julio and she always introduced him as her son-in-law, but the rumor mill was that she didn't have a daughter or step daughter for that matter.

What she did have was money. At least more than anybody I personally knew, and Julio was there to make sure that money stayed there. He would certainly make sure it would be in his personal account when the old hag kicked the bucket. They lived on the entire second floor and ran a beauty parlor at street level. We knew Julio was really her current boyfriend but everybody just played her game.

"...And this is the kitchen on your right..." the landlady was saying as they came by the open doorway.

"Oh my goodness! That smells good! What are you cooking?" She saw me standing by the stove.

"Good morning Mrs. Pawlak, I'm afraid you are a little late for breakfast" I said working my toothpick and putting away the plates on the drip rack.

"Damn!" She said short-jabbing an invisible punch bag.

I had forced myself to get up early this morning. Being a Sunday, I knew I had the entire kitchen to myself at least until mid-morning before other tenants would wander into the kitchen.

"This is..." she said glancing at her companions and pointing in my direction, I noticed a brief hesitation as if trying to remember my name, however, regaining her composure swiftly finished with "one of my tenants."

A man and a woman dressed in what appeared to be a Salvation Army uniform stood just behind Mrs. Pawlak at a military attention.

I waved a greeting which they acknowledged by an imperceptible head nod.

I took a quick second look at the couple. The man must have been in his early forties and had an uncanny resemblance to Tommy Lee Jones. The woman, much older and petite, looked vaguely like Mother Theresa.

Mrs. Pawlak turned on her heels and continued down the hallway to room number five shadowed by the two figures. "Most unusual new tenants," I thought. "Mrs. Pawlak does not take couples." I decided to linger in the kitchen a little longer to find out more about the new arrivals.

I washed and cleaned the old and pockmarked aluminum pots and pans that had certainly seen better days in their previous lives, and that now I shared with the other tenants, two other tenants to be exact. Old Bernie the retired alcoholic from room one and Carl the carpenter from four. I had no problem staying in room two next to old Bernie. His only bad habit, besides drinking, was to talk to himself and come and go at odd times. The room nobody wanted was number three, across the kitchen and next to the shower and bathroom that we all shared.

"... Think it will be suitable," Tommy Lee Jones was saying.

"And we love that it is close to the train station." Mother Theresa piped in.

"No shit." I thought. "Any closer and WE would be the train station."

"...probably this evening," Tommy said.

"Or if it is more convenient for you..." Mother Theresa started.

"Oh, no. No problem," Mrs. Pawlak cut in. "This evening is fine."

The voices faded down the hallway, past the laundry room and up the stairway.

That same evening, while doing my laundry and reviewing my calculus homework, the door up the stairway squeaked open, breaking my concentration. Three silhouettes stood momentarily against the brighter background.

"Watch your step." said Tommy Lee Jones.

"Let me go in first." Mother Theresa trailed in.

The odd couple was back.

Down the steps, under the dim light I noticed Mother Theresa leading by the hand a younger man in dark shades. He held in his right hand a red and white collapsible walking cane, Tommy Lee Jones trailing behind carried two heavy suitcases.

A few minutes later only the odd couple returned, this time exiting the basement through the side entrance.

Two days later, after returning from school, I was planning to study for a couple more hours at least until midnight. I headed for the kitchen. I needed strong coffee to get me going.

I turned the light on.

"Holly shit...I'm sorry I didn't know ..." I jumped back.

Sitting right there at the table, in what had been complete darkness and silence, was the new tenant eating a well prepared meal.

"You must be..." I stammered, hesitating to finish with "crazy", "the new tenant" or "out of your mind."

No response.

He continued eating undisturbed, swallowed, picked a napkin, cleaned his hands and lips, and slowly stood up.

"Raul Santos." He said extending his hand in my direction. He must have been in his late thirties, dark complexion, perhaps a tad taller than I was and obviously Hispanic.

"Gino," I said shaking his hand across the table, "Gino Briseno from room three."

"Sorry about the light." He said returning to his chair. "I must have forgotten to turn it on." He spoke with a slight accent I could not put my finger on. He tilted his head slightly back as he spoke and under the dim light I could see a horrific scar across his face that ran from his left cheek, cut through his upper lip, and ended just below his right jaw. But most remarkable were his eyes or rather the lack of, just two huge empty sockets remained where the eyes should have been.

"Not... a problem." I said, trying to downplay my surprise. He must have sensed this because with a swift motion he reached for his sunglasses in his breast pocket and put them on.

"I lost my eyesight a few years back." He said in an apologetic tone. "By the way, I am done cooking, feel free to use the stove." He said returning to his meal.

"Thanks, I just need a cup of coffee." I said as I fumbled in the dish rack for a teacup.

"You must be the student the old man was telling me about."

I pulled a chair across the table. "Oh, you met old Bernie, yes I am attending U of I, but I also have a part time job on the North-side." I sat down.

"So, how did it happen?"

He glanced in my direction. "Happened, what?"

"Your eyes, how did you lose your eyesight?"

He continued eating for what seemed like a long time and for a moment I regretted my stupid question. "I'm sorry..." I started.

"No, it's all right." He said with a wave of a hand. "It is a long story, perhaps some other time."

With that I understood that the conversation was over. I retrieved my coffee from the microwave and left.

In the ensuing weeks, whenever we ran into each other we would exchange a few pleasantries. But, there was an odd and uneasy feeling I had about his attitude and demeanor I could not explain. Needless to say I tried to avoid him at all costs. He would spend hours in the kitchen cooking. It was amazing to see him, cut, chop vegetables, slice steaks, marinate them, spice them, and check the stove flame, none of the other tenants cooked as much or as fancy as he did.

He would come out and sit on the steps of the side walk for hours at a time staring into empty space. The odd couple would come to pick him up twice a week, disappear for hours and return late at night.

One day, it must have been a holiday because I wasn't at school. I was cooking the usual, fried eggs with corned beef. He strolled in carrying three or four shopping bags. By now, I am sure; he knew who was in the kitchen just by the smell of the food.

"Hey Gino, I want to ask you something." He said even before setting the bags on the table. But his voice was a little different today, as if chewing on marbles.

"Shoot." I said somewhat puzzled, since he wasn't the social or talkative type. Then I noticed his legs were wobbling.

"I bought two shirts today and I want you to tell me what color they are." He said pulling open two packages. The other bag had a full unopened six pack. It was the first time I'd seen him drink.

"Sure, no problem,"

That unusual request got me thinking. Why did he care about the colors if he could not see them? Perhaps he did care how he was perceived by others, who knows? I was debating these thoughts in my head when he said. "I like the light tones. Nothing flashy that attracts attention, you know what I mean?"

"Yeah, I know." I lied.

"I asked the lady at the store for one light blue, and the other one light brown." He opened the other bag and placed the six pack on the table. "They go with mostly any pants color, especially black." He had already opened the packages and was feeling the cloth quality.

The colors came pretty close to what he wanted. But, this was food for thought: If the shirts were exchanged for bright neon orange or bright red...hmm, wait, no need for that, how about if I just told him that all his shirts and pants were bright red...That would be evil.

"So, you do remember your colors well, huh?" I ventured trying to sound casual.

Trains, pause.

The Chicago Transit Authority trains raced overhead. "The El", ran from Cicero to The Loop at about fifteen minute time intervals during the day, peaking up during rush hour, and then dying slowly far in between into the night. Living close to "The El" you grew accustomed to pausing your conversation while the trains went by.

"Yeah, I was just like everybody else. But one day...hey you want a beer?" He was already ripping open the six pack and handing me a can.

"I'm sorry, I really don't..."

"You have no choice" he wasn't smiling.

"Okay."

He took a long sip and leaned on his chair.

"I was dating this girl, and somehow, one day she ended up pregnant. She wanted to get married. But, I wasn't sure. I really liked her a lot, trust me, but as a girlfriend. I didn't want to get married, I was young! And the last thing I wanted was to be tied to somebody or anybody forever. But there was something else too; a friend of mine had seen her leaving the restaurant she worked for with somebody else. So now the question was, maybe she was lying about being pregnant or if she was, maybe the baby wasn't mine. What do you think?" He drained the can and opened the next.

"Well, yeah, you're right." I had to agree. "But, did you ask her?"

Trains, pause.

"Of course I asked her. And the bitch denied everything. So I started following her and sure enough, she was seeing somebody else behind my back. A couple days later they went to a park, and when they started kissing I couldn't stand it anymore. I always carried a gun under the driver's seat, you know." He made a swift motion mimicking the action.

"I wanted to kill them both right there and then. But there were too many people around and I didn't want to take any chances, you know."

"Well, it wasn't necessary to do anything, just walk away or forget about it, especially if she was pregnant and what if the baby was indeed yours?" I said nursing my beer and just trying to say something.

"NOOOO!" He screamed banging his fist on the table so hard that the empty cans tumbled to the floor. Why in hell did I have to say something so stupid?

"IT WASN'T MINE! IT WAS HIS! SHE DESERVED TO DIE, SHE HAD TO PAY! She was cheating on me. Why? I... loved her, I did." His yelling and screaming was now turning into pleading and crying. "You know that she had to die, right?" He was now wiping imaginary tears from imaginary eyes.

I was now speechless and my knuckles had turned white clamped shut on the edge of the table to keep my hands from shaking. I didn't want to know anymore.

"Please, tell me I did the right thing, because both...PIGS... HAD TO DIE! THEY HAD TO PAY!" It was uncanny the sudden change in his demeanor, almost like the overlapping voice of that of the victims and that of the executioner.

"TELL MEEEEE!" He was standing now and leaning in my direction across the table, two dark, cavernous voids inches from my face. My mouth was dry and try as I might words just would not come out.

His semi-empty overturned beer was slowly spilling on the table.

Trains, pause.

"Ye...yes, you're right." I finally said. But he couldn't hear me!

His mouth was opening and closing.

Finally the train faded in the distance.

"Yes, yes, you are right!" I repeated.

He returned to his chair, clasped both hands on the table and in a very soft voice said, "Thank you." He opened another can and drank half of it, leaned back on the chair, crossed his leg and, as if nothing had happened, continued. "A couple of days later after they died I was stopped by the cops. They took me to the police station and asked me a bunch of questions, but I'm telling you, they had nothing on me. They even searched my car and found nothing, so they had to let me go. I couldn't leave town right away because I was waiting for this money from the construction company." He paused briefly to drink some more.

By now I was sorry and terrified I had ever asked him for the story, and I was realizing too late that I didn't want to know anymore. This was my chance. "I, I have to go" I said. Trying to sound apprehensive and got up.

"SIT DOWN!" he screamed. "I'M NOT DONE YET."

I sat down.

"I didn't know Karen had two brothers." He continued. "That lived in Sacramento, only a couple hours away. When I came face to face with them, it was dark. My apartment was on the second floor. They were waiting for me in the parking lot. I was getting out of the car. I heard my name and turned around. I remember seeing the flashes then the pain of the first three or four bullets, then nothing."

He breathed a long pause, now I was afraid of saying something, anything for that matter, much less the stupid question of "Did you die?" But it did occur to me.

"I was in a coma for three days at the hospital; I woke up ten days after. I had shattered bones, busted lungs, kidney failure, you name it. It took countless operations to sew me up and put me back together. None of the doctors gave me much of a chance to live. They had removed twelve bullets from my body. I told them I could not believe I had been shot twelve times and still be alive. The doctor said the police had bullet thirteen. It had not been lodged in my body because it had gone thru my temple, fired at point blank range, and out the other side, blowing both eyes in the process."

Now I needed a drink! I was riveted to the chair. I could not deny it was brutal and he had the scars to prove it.

The entire house shook again, the trains overhead racing to meet some insane deadline were getting far in between as the night grew darker.

"It is a miracle you survived." I ventured, fearing any comment may set him up again.

He didn't say anything for a long time and just stared into empty space. But now I wanted to know.

"What happened with the brothers afterwards? Did they get arrested? You know, after all, you could identify them."

"Are you making fun of me? His scar by the cheek seemed to twitch on its own.

"No, no...I mean you knew their names." Not again, me and my big mouth.

"The police interviewed them but never charged them with anything. I never mentioned their names, in fact, later when the police did have evidence and asked me to press charges for attempted murder I refused. I told them they were not the ones."

"How come?"

"Don't you get it? Attempted murder carries very little jail time! No, no, the bastards did not attempt to murder me! They killed me! THEY HAD TO PAY!" He was now dragging his words.

"It took me a while..." he was breathing hard. "Maybe one day I will tell you the details, but all I can say right now is that they did pay...and where they went there is no such thing as parole." Now I was just getting a glimpse into his mind. He drank the last of his beer, grabbed his bags and mumbling something he disappeared down the hallway.

The rumble of a solitary train receded in the distance and into the dead of the night.

"Good morning Gino." The voice said behind me. "I haven't seen you for the last three days!"

"Hi Bernie, I have been busy at work and school."

"Have you seen..." he glanced at the end of the hallway and mimicked a walking cane.

"No, I..."

He moved his finger over his lips and waved me to follow him.

"He's been a pain in everybody's ass." He said once we were in his room. "He had an argument with Carl the carpenter the other day, something about pots and pans left in the sink, you know, stupid things. But they were pretty close to beating each other up." He rolled his eyes.

"I try to stay away from him as much as I can, did he say anything to you?"

Bernie combed his nonexistent hair with his fingers. "Yesterday I was in the kitchen and he started yelling at me. He was accusing me of taking his stuff from the refrigerator. He said that next time he is going to deal with me. I don't know what he meant by it. I told him I did not know anything and left in a hurry."

"Should we tell Mrs. Pawlak about it?" I wondered out loud.

He shrugged. "No, he hasn't done anything criminal yet."

I wanted to tell Bernie right then and there that this miserable blind was a criminal on the run! Was I the only one who knew his past? A chill ran down my spine.

"Bernie, what do you know about him?"

"Well... not much, just what he told to Carl and me, that in a car accident, his family died, he was paralyzed and blind and he has been in therapy since." Bernie must have seen my face going white. "What, do you know something I don't?"

"Listen to me Bernie. Just don't talk to him, if you see him, run the other way." I could not trust Bernie, he would start bubbling the real story to anybody, and then we all would be in big trouble.

"You are making a big deal out of it, like I said it was just a stupid thing. Come on Gino, for God's sake he's blind!" His wrinkles dug deeper around his smile and shrugging he dismissed the subject.

When the weekend came two days later I was still thinking about it. I had to warn Carl the carpenter but he was again out of town on his construction projects. It would be days if not weeks before I could talk to him.

I had to talk to Mrs. Pawlak, but, what was I going to tell her? How about if what he told me was a lie? Now, wasn't she supposed to run a criminal check on all tenants?

Hell no. I had to go tell her.

Twice I went up to the top step, and twice I came down.

What if Bernie was right? "This was getting ridiculous." My teeth were grinding. Gathering all my courage, I climbed the steps for the third time and out to the front. The glass front door displayed the marks and scars of one too many unloved stickers. Up above the peeling paint a flickering neon sign read "Salon Unisex." The first half of the second word was out; I wondered if it was an advertising gimmick.

"You want me to do what?" Mrs. Pawlak's disdain was obvious. "What if I run a criminal check on you? What would I find out if I did? Huh?" Her eyes drilled me up and down.

I wanted to yell in her face, "go ahead witch do it." But I did not want to upset her in any way. Not now, I knew we were in real danger, I had to insist some more.

"Like I said he is causing problems and it is not just me. Maybe he does drugs, who knows? Can you ask or get some references from the people that brought him in?" I immediately realized how stupid it sounded.

"Did I ask you for references?" Her words dripped out with bile. "Now, he hasn't done anything. Tell me. Why should I call the cops, huh?"

"Well I think..."

"Do me a favor and stop thinking. Now, if you'll excuse me..." Her skeletal figure quickly disappeared behind a curtain.

I headed back to my room cursing thru my teeth. Bernie's room was closed and dark, nothing unusual, he was probably still out with his drinking friends. I looked down the hallway past the kitchen, dark, no music from room five; I thought the coast was clear.

I went in the kitchen, drank from my water bottle in the fridge.

Suddenly a voice thundered on the doorway.

"HEY! WHO PUT THIS CHAIR IN MY WAY?" I jumped out and water splashed. Out of nowhere the blind was standing there moving a chair to the side.

"I...don't..." I put a hand on my mouth but it was too late!

"Gino? Is that you?" His voice was now softer, inviting.

Silence.

"I know it is you. You did it on purpose didn't you? You wanted me to trip and break a leg. Huh?" He was now walking slowly in my direction and his voice was rising again. "Or maybe you wanted me to trip and hit my head. Was that your plan, Gino?"

I tiptoed around the large wooden table. Now I was at the farthest end from the door.

In the blink of an eye a butcher knife from the wooden block was shining in his hand. "Come on Gino, talk to me." He pointed and thrust the knife into the empty air where I had been only seconds before. He then retracted quickly to cover my only escape. For a second I thought the pounding from my chest would give me away.

"I know you're right here and you're going to pay."

He was now circling back on the other side of the table, but still intercepting the door. I had to think fast! I picked up a chair and flung it at him across the table. The back of the chair smashed with a sickening thud right across his face and tumbled to the floor.

He barely flinched.

He kept coming and his face was twitching with rage. I swept another chair and hurled it in his direction. He dove over the table, the slicing blade missing my chest by inches. I tripped and landed on the floor against the wall. The chair smashed on the other side above the sink splintering glass and knocking pots and pans. He rolled down the table and sprung up swinging left and right. I laid there motionless, holding my breath. Blood from a gash on his face ran down his chin, hit the floor and tiny droplets sprayed on my left arm. The pots and pans crashing on the floor had briefly distracted him, now he wasn't sure where I was. He wasn't cursing anymore. He was growling, wild, sniffing. I looked up, his face, the blackness of those voids, was like a skull dancing with a corpse. He sniffed again, scanned, trying to pick up the scent.

I was frozen with terror, unable to move.

Suddenly a door slammed at the far entrance to the basement. He ran to the hallway and yelled at the top of his lungs. "I'm going to get you mother f...er!"

He stepped back in the kitchen and let out a long and painful wailing and then discharged his fury, stabbing again and again the wooden table. Before going to his room he picked up a chair and smashed it against the wall.

I did not dare to move until I heard the door from his room slam shut. I had to restrain myself from flying out of the kitchen. I tiptoed around the debris and once in the hallway I ran out. I did not see anybody by the entrance but whatever it was that had slammed the door had certainly saved my life.

The beauty shop was closed. A side door lead to Mrs. Pawlak's apartment on the second floor.

"What do you want?" Boyfriend Julio, beer in hand, answered the door.

"Who is it honey?" The quacking came from far inside, before I could answer.

"You have to come down! He's gone crazy, attacked me and is breaking everything!" I said out-loud for her to hear me.

"Easy! Slow down! What are you talking about?" said Gorilla with beer.

"The blind, the blind from room five." I was trying to calm myself down.

"Honey, why don't you go down and see what's happening, I'll be there in a minute." Mrs. Pawlak was now at the door in pajamas and sandals.

I followed gorilla with beer downstairs, feeling safer behind his massive frame.

"What the..." He gasped at the sight of broken glass, overturned furniture and the butcher knife jabbed on the table. "Did he do this?" I just nodded and pointed down the hallway. He took another sip from the can. Shoved his spilling belly back in his pants and headed down to room five.

As much as I wanted to listen to their conversation I was not going to get any closer than that and I was ready to bail out. I could not make heads or tails of what they were saying. But suddenly there was loud cursing from both sides, then a scuffle, muffled sounds and glass breaking.

Mrs. Pawlak came running. Now it sounded like a tornado in room five. "Oh dear God, oh my God!" She went past the kitchen.

I tried to stop her. "No, don't..." too late. She went straight to the room door. "Please honey stop it, don't hurt him!"

Just then the door flung open and a tumbleweed of legs and arms almost ran her over. The door slammed behind. The tumbleweed slowly stood up. "Oh honey, what happened to you?" Only pieces of shirt hung from one shoulder and gorilla without beer was bleeding heavily from his nose and mouth.

The door flung open again and a lamp came crashing spraying glass everywhere.

"Come on! Don't you just stand there?" Mrs. Pawlak was flailing her arms to get my attention. "Do something!"

I turned on my heels and flew the scene. I did not stop until I was about a block away at a gas station and from there I called the cops. By the time I got back, a police cruiser, lights flashing, was parked in front. I stood there across the street where curious bystanders had started gathering. A second patrol arrived and two more cops went in. Two minutes later two more cruisers from opposite sides of the street with wailing sirens screeched to a halt and four more cops went in.

"The gang bangers got busted." A middle aged man in a wife-beater and sandals was saying.

"Yeah it was about time," said a lady carrying grocery bags. "I think they are the ones that killed those two people on 18th street." She looked at me for approval.

I didn't know what to answer but she was already looking across the street. "Look!" There was a hush in the crowd.

The blind; shirtless, barefooted and completely covered in blood was carried out by four police officers to a waiting ambulance, four more disheveled officers trailed behind.

"He must be the gang ring-leader." The man in the wife beater said.

"Yeah, but where are the others?" said another.

"I think they are all dead," quacked the lady with the grocery bags.

"Hey! You," an old and tall guy with white hair and a piercing glance was pointing at me. "Don't you also live over there?"

Now heads were turning and fingers pointing.

"No, I... don't." I started to walk away.

"Yes!" The lady with the grocery bags was looking at me. "I think I've seen him with the others." I had to get out of Dodge and fast.

The following day, after spending the night at a friend's house, where I intended to move immediately, I went to pick up my stuff and get my security deposit from Mrs. Pawlak.

"That miserable blind is not putting a foot in this house anymore!" She said when I asked about him. "I'm going to make sure he rots in jail forever." She was fuming.

"Is he in jail now?"

"No. He is in the hospital but he is under arrest for disorderly conduct, aggravated battery and destruction of property, plus, resisting arrest. I cannot believe it took six cops to restrain him. But there is more, one of those cops that were here yesterday called this morning. He said the blind was on parole after serving close to fifteen years in jail for murdering two people."

"Two people?" a chill ran down my spine. It was true, and he had never been charged for the other two.

"Yes, it gives me the creeps." She said shaking. "He killed not one, but two, can you believe it? I did not know anything about it. Thank God they're coming to pick up his stuff today." She rolled her eyes.

"Mrs. Pawlak," I said coyly. "I... I'm moving out and I need my security deposit to..."

"You need what? You have the nerve to ask me for your deposit when you are the one that started all this?" She was back being her own self. "Tell me who is going to pay for the broken china, furniture, fix the walls, huh?"

"I didn't do it, it was..."

"Don't give me that crap." Her bony finger swung in my direction. "I am doing you a favor by not telling the cops that you were involved. You should be glad I'm not pressing charges." The door slammed before I could stammer something else.

I could do nothing but grind my teeth in desperation. The witch was stealing my money!

My head was spinning. A splitting headache with only one thought.

SHE HAD TO PAY!

Trains, pause.

THE CURSE OF THE NECRONOMICON

The antique shop was almost hidden from view. A stairway flanked by a weathered metal fence led potential customers to the underground level below the Cafe de Anzur, a Turkish restaurant that tended to the writers, painters and self-proclaimed philosophers that either lectured at the nearby University or peddled alms on the street corner.

Dennis Miller was neither one of them, he always thought of himself as a mathematician, but for most people he was just a semiretired math teacher that, just to kill time, taught calculus at the local high school in his home town thirty miles away.

He glanced across the town square, the clock on the tower marked ten forty five, he double checked with his wristwatch. He had almost an hour to spare before his meeting at the Cafe with Richard, a young and brilliant Chemistry professor he had met just before his retirement, some four years ago during his teaching days.

The antique shop sign, true to its name, hung precariously by two stubborn nails above the wooden door. He did not remember seeing the shop before, granted he was not a regular at the Cafe, but had been there quite a few times. He had always prided himself on his photographic memory, God forbid he was losing it. In any case, this was a good time to check it out. A small sign by the door said "open". Dennis pushed the heavy and weathered door that squeaked on its hinges and rattled a wind chime that hung from a rusty chain.

"Hello?"

A single fluorescent light hung from the ceiling and cast a pale hue to the bric-a-brac on the shelves that lined the walls.

No answer.

African masks and carved ivory tusks piled the center displays, by a center column and under two medieval shields stood a knight armor holding a sword to the chest. Other medieval weapons hung from the walls and torcher devices from the same era were cordoned off to keep the curious and the daring out of harm's way.

"Hello?"

The place seemed deserted.

A long glass cabinet farther down caught his attention. Inside, among other things, stood a skull riddled with bullet holes, it rested over a piece of paper with a caption that he was unable to read in the dim light. Next to it there was a smaller skull, about the size of a fist, again he could barely make the writings but he could make the price which he noticed was higher than the one of the larger skull.

"It is genuine and in excellent condition." A voice called behind his back.

Dennis caught himself barely able to restrain a scream; his hand was on his chest. He turned and saw a thin man of short stature in oriental robes "You scared the hell..."

"I am sorry if I startled you," the antique dealer said. "My name is Derazahl Al Udba. How can I help you?" His eyes were almost hidden from view by the red turban he wore and the rest of his facial features covered by a white beard that reached to his chest.

"I'm... I'm just looking" Dennis said trying to distance himself from the cabinet and momentarily taken aback by the, perhaps unintended, comical appearance of his host.

"That is perfectly fine" the old man said.

He had walked around the glass cabinet and was pulling the large skull over the counter.

"This" he said pointing between the black eye sockets, "is the skull of Pancho Villa" he reverently made the sign of the cross. "But, for only two hundred dollars can be yours."

Dennis wondered how many more were there in the storage room.

"What about the small one?"

"Ah, very good, the small one, this one..." he said holding it up to the light with extreme care, "is only five hundred dollars." he seemed fascinated.

"How come?"

The antique dealer put a finger over his mouth and whispered. "This one is when Pancho Villa was a baby."

"What?" Dennis was looking into the stone face of Derazahl Al Udba. "Are you kidding me?"

The antique dealer exploded in a mad scientist laugh.

"Of course I'm kidding you." He finally said when both had managed to stop laughing. "Can I ask what you do for a living?" he inquired in a more serious tone.

"I'm a mathematician" Dennis said more at easy.

"Ah, a connoisseur!"

The antique dealer glanced at the mini-me skull still in his hand. "You don't need this." He tossed it over his shoulder and rested a friendly hand over Dennis' back. Glass shattered in the back where the mini-me landed leaving a trail of broken bric-a-brac. "You might be interested in one of the most unusual items I have ever come across in my life" He motioned Dennis down the hallway.

The antique dealer stopped at a wall where a life size Samurai warrior was ready to strike a massive brass gong; he reached between the Samurai legs and pulled out a long handle. The Samurai screamed and let go of the striker with all its might. Instinctively Dennis went for his ears; there was only a muffled "thud" and part of the wall swung open.

"I still get a kick out of this, believe me." The antique dealer smiled as he climbed inside a secret and well-lit office. "Please come in"

Behind a painting a safe materialized. As he ran the combination, the safe opened and inside, was an ancient flat wooden box with rusted metal guards on every corner. He set it up on a table.

"What you are about to witness is the last remaining copy of the real and original *Necronomicon.*" He stood there like an actor waiting for a standing ovation.

"Necro... what?" Dennis was mystified.

The antique dealer's jaw dropped and his disgust was evident. He raised his hands. "That's it!" He quickly picked up the box and placed it back in the safe. "Go, go you cannot stay." The wall was swinging back in place. Once they were out, the antique dealer led Dennis out of the shop.

"Forget what you saw and don't ever come back." The door slammed shut.

Dennis was rattled by the sudden attitude change of the Arab, maybe it was part of his mystic and eccentricity.

The Cafe de Anzur was crowded now and he was going to be lucky if he secured a table anytime soon. He was resigned to wait when he spotted his friend Richard already sitting at a table.

"Problem finding a parking spot?" Richard sipped from his glass.

"No, I took the train today. Listen I have a question for you."

"Shoot."

"What do you know about a book called Necro-something?"

"I didn't know you were into the occult."

"No, I'm not; you know I don't believe any of that nonsense... I overheard a conversation, I'm just curious."

"The book's name is The Necronomicon." Richard said. "It is allegedly the most terrible of the magical grimoires of all time; it contains ancient spells, invocations, detailed instructions on how to summon the dead or even the devil himself, exorcisms and rituals on how to control and harness secret and powerful forces."

"Wow! Quite a book, it sounds like a sorcerer's treasure." Dennis' mind was reeling.

"There's only one problem."

"What's that?"

"The book does not exist."

"But...You said it..."

"Allegedly...The book, or rather the title, was simply a figment of imagination of Howard Philip Lovecraft an American writer from the 1920's and relatively unknown in his own time. In his horror short stories he made repeated reference to this imaginary book, soon other writers jumped on the bandwagon citing excerpts and passages from the dreadful Necronomicon. However, long before his death in 1937, he officially declared that the book and his alleged author, one mad Arab by the name of Abdul Alhazred that lived in the seventh century were fictitious and without a doubt his own creation."

Dennis was mesmerized by the turn of events. "Isn't it possible that this... Lovecraft was in fact in possession of the book or at least had access to it, then downplayed the significance?"

"Hardly, I think he was telling the truth, first of all; there is no mention of this book anywhere before his writings. Second; any human being in possession of a book of this magnitude and caliber would reap untold riches, fame and fortune. Lovecraft died unknown and penniless under the care of two old Aunts of his."

They ordered their meals, but Dennis' appetite had vanished. "So, we can only conclude that the book does not exist." He said a little disappointed.

"Look Dennis I'm just showing you the tip of the iceberg, there is a lot more to it than we can discuss in one day, as a matter of fact you can go to the bookstore right now and buy the latest edition of The Necronomicon."

"Are you kidding me? I thought you said it did not exist."

"Fakes, Dennis, fakes."

"Oh, I see."

"You know, sooner or later someone was bound to realize; hey, if there isn't one let's write one, right? Well, there are several versions out there, can I say totally useless? Yes I can." Richard said digging into his meal.

"How do you know so much about this subject? Dennis was curious.

"Now I'm returning your question, I didn't know you were into the occult."

"Remember, we Chemists are the new version of the ancient Alchemists." Richard said matter of fact.

"You're not trying to transmute lead into gold are you?"

"Oh no, not at all," Richard was smiling.

"I really appreciate your magnificent dissertation professor Richard. As another soul has been saved from the darkness of ignorance and illuminated with the light of your wisdom." Dennis bowed as the submissive disciple.

"Save it for your unlucky students old timer." Richard said with a wave of his hand. "Okay, what do you have for me?" They had finished their meal and the waiter was collecting the plates.

Dennis retrieved a manila envelope from his briefcase. "Your mathematical model is right on the money." He pulled two pages crammed with formulae and graphics. "Save for a slight deviation at Maxima of point one where second derivative of F of g equals zero." He turned the pages. "I have a summary of possible outcomes but I must say that this is just theoretical and highly speculative. According to my calculations it would take massive and expensive equipment just to prove the feasibility..." He was leafing through more notes.

"You mean, like this?" Richard was unfolding a wide roll of paper across the table.

The computer printout was cryptic to the untrained eye; a blue water mark ran the length of each page. "Restricted access-Do not remove from lab." And at the bottom in fine print it read, *The Einstein Project.* Dennis was not a computer expert but he could tell almost immediately that this was the initial stage of the experiment.

"I'll be damned! I can't believe they're doing it" He was looking into Richard eyes, "Is this for real?"

"You better believe it, it held for one billionth of a second!" He almost tore the printout from Dennis' hand and stashed it back into his briefcase.

"Sorry I'm not supposed to show this to anybody."

"This is amazing! Just the discovery of the process could revolutionize the entire history of mankind! But tell me who else is involved in this?"

"I can't say anything, I am not even supposed to tell you anything, now promise me..." He closed an imaginary zipper over his mouth.

"Okay, I will not share it with my dog. But, I'm curious how you managed to maintain synchronicity in the..."

"I am not at liberty to say, look I got to run back to the lab." He clasped his briefcase, collected his trench coat from the chair next to him and waved Dennis' notes. "Thanks, I'll call you" and disappeared into the street.

Dennis stood there trying to process the dissimilar events. The lunch crowd was thinning out, he got up and thankfully he had enough time to clear out a nagging question. A thin rain had begun to fall and passersby were hurrying for cover. He crossed the square and using his briefcase he managed to keep his head partially dry.

The bookstore did not seem to have a particular book arrangement as one may have expected, science fiction books stood next to *Mexican Cuisine for Dummies* and *Big Foot; New Revelations From a Shoemaker.* When Dennis finally managed to locate an attendant, the teenager said, "If you don't see it we don't have it."

"But, can you help me look for it?"

The teenager shrugged and smiled. "Are you kidding? Look I have other customers to attend to," and before Dennis said abracadabra the teenager was gone. "Well, it looks like it's one of that find-it-at-your-own-risk type of deal." He said to himself. He was ready to give up after perusing through several racks when he heard a deep voice behind him.

"Are you looking for anything in particular?"

Dennis turned.

An impeccably dressed gentleman stood there holding a clipboard in one hand and a walking cane under his arm. For a moment Dennis hesitated and almost felt silly to ask for a book that everybody knew was a fake.

"Yes, as a matter of fact I do, do you carry a book by the name *The Necronomicon?*"

The man smiled. "Yes we do, please follow me."

The man led the way to the far end of the store.

Dennis related the early exchange with the young attendant hoping the insensitive employee would merely get a reprimand and improve his social skills.

"Oh I'm sorry, I will personally take care of it and, believe me, it will never happen again."

He reached for the upper shelf, and without reading the title, handed it to Dennis.

"It is just for a research paper." said Dennis as a way of excuse.

"Certainly" the man scribbled a note on the clipboard.

Dennis opened the book and instinctively checked the edition number and the year published. He then looked at the dust jacket at the back of the book ... he noticed a small white rectangle with five numbers instead of a bar-code and ten-digit ISBN number. He removed the dust jacket and looked at the back lower right corner by the spine; the book had an almost invisible indented mark.

He turned to face the manager /owner. "This is a Book-of-the-Month Club edition..."

The man was gone.

Dennis looked behind the adjacent shelves. He was sure he would have seen or heard the man leave. Well, in any case he had the book and he was ready to do some reading on his way back home.

Two weeks later he was back in town. Even though he did not have a meeting with Richard, he was here for another reason. He got off at the train station. It was early and instead of the usual taxicab he would take the slower bus ride downtown.

He strolled to the newsstand next to the bus stop, the headlines on the local newspaper caught his attention; "LOCAL TEENAGER FOUND DEAD." The inset picture showed a somewhat familiar face but he could not place it. He bought the paper just in time to make it to the departing bus.

The details of the gruesome death were horrifying, but more chilling were how the body parts had been arranged at a crossroads in a wooded area and strange symbols drawn in blood encircled the scene.

He almost missed his stop at the Town Square.

Now he knew who the inset picture was.

The bookstore was crowded; he pushed his way to the counter and held the paper in front of the young woman tending the cash register.

"Is him, right? The startled clerk did not answer but switched her gaze from the picture to the customers then down to the open drawer.

"IS HIM, RIGHT?" He was yelling now and almost rubbing the paper in her face.

This time she nodded and turned away with tears swelling in her eyes.

"Hey mister!" Some customers were pulling and tagging at his coat; he freed himself from the crowd and exited the bookstore.

He crossed the Plaza to Cafe de Anzur and walked down the steps to the antique shop, the tilted sign said open. He pushed the door, the chimes and the squeaking hinges announced his presence.

"Please come in" Derazahl Al Udba did not turn from the table where he was examining an ancient manuscript under a magnifying glass.

"What can I do for you?"

"I'm not interested in The Necronomicon."

"What? Not you again" He was facing Dennis. "Are you coming just to tell me that you are not interested in a book you do not know anything about?"

"I know everything about it, because I read it."

"If you did you read a fake one."

"They're all fakes."

"Ah! Now we are beginning to understand each other." He motioned Dennis to a chair.

Dennis tossed the paper in front of the antique dealer. "What do you know about this?" The gruesome headline was shouting from the paper.

"I read about it, and it is unfortunate that even in a small town like ours crimes like this occur."

"I am talking about the way it was carried out, The Modus Operandi or M.O. as the police would say."

"It is strange indeed, perhaps a serial killer landed in our midst."

"This was a satanic ritual just like it is described in The Necronomicon."

"The paper does not make any reference to Satanic..."

"Maybe they don't, but I'm sure it is. You know how the police hold certain information during the investigation." Dennis retrieved the paper. "Logan, Peter Logan, the kid worked at the bookstore across the street. Did you know him?"

"No, I never met him. The paper doesn't say where he worked, how do you know?"

"Last time I was here I bought a book from him or rather from his boss the manager."

"Oh yes, I know Mrs. Rothschild, nice lady."

"Well, It wasn't a lady of that I'm sure." Dennis had a bad feeling about this. "That's strange. Do you know of any local group or cult involved in witchcraft or Kabbalistic rituals? "

"Not that I am aware of, but why are you asking me all these questions?"

Dennis opened his briefcase and pulled out a book, he tossed it on the table, "page sixty six, and sixth paragraph."

The antique dealer shrugged in disdain at such cheap and blatant fakery.

"I take it this is the book you bought."

Dennis pointed a finger to it.

Reluctantly the antique dealer opened the book, found the page and ran his finger down to the sixth paragraph and began to read.

"The offering shall be separated from the head... the protective circle in the house of Orus drawn in blood... where two roads cross...to summon

The Lord of Darkness at the stroke of midnight during a full moon." He paused. "Are you saying someone is using the book?"

"Exactly, and maybe not just this worthless fake."

The antique dealer bolted in the direction of the secret swinging wall, Dennis heard the samurai scream and a few minutes later Derazahl Al Udba came dragging his feet holding an empty and ancient wooden box.

"Stolen, it was stolen!" he was crying.

"You had it last time I was here."

"I'm not sure, I never opened the box. Last time I saw it was with Julius my assistant."

"Why would he steal it when he could buy one for a few dollars across the street?"

"THIS book is priceless and extremely dangerous in the wrong hands." The antique dealer was staring into the empty box.

"I thought you said they were all fakes."

"Not this one," he paused and looked Dennis in the eye then crossed his fingers and lowered his voice as if what he was about to disclose was only for the initiated and under no circumstances should be revealed to the layman. "Unbeknownst to H.P. Lovecraft the book did exist and had existed for many centuries guarded in most secrecy by a secret sect within the Catholic Church."

"I understand that there had been no references to The Necronomicon before Lovecraft." Dennis pointed out.

"That is correct, because the book's name is NOT *The Necronomicon* .The real name is <u>O Antigo Livro de Sao Cipriano</u> or The Great Book of Saint Cyprian."

"Never heard of it."

"Don't feel bad, most people haven't." He leaned over the table. "Saint Cyprian, long before he was a saint or a monk for that matter, was one of the most gifted Magicians and feared Sorcerers of all time. He lived around the 7th Century A.D., now modern Portugal.

Legend has it that he had a pact with the devil. He possessed untold wealth, nobility titles, castles and fertile lands. One day he got a glimpse of a beautiful young nun from the nearby convent. He was so taken by her beauty that he vowed to make her his wife. His courting advances were met with polite but firm refusal.

Justina, the young nun, made it clear that her life was dedicated to serve God and under no circumstances would change her mind. Cyprian was furious, accustomed to have his most bizarre whims fulfilled, this was unthinkable. He had promised her a lavish palace with maids and servants, jewelry, and nobility to no avail. But he had one more card up his sleeve; sorcery.

He summoned the Angel of Darkness, the most powerful of the evil forces above the incubus, succubus and lesser demons. From a cloud of Sulfur a voice said. "Your request shall come to pass."

The more the Devil tried to tempt Justina the more she prayed. Eventually even the Devil had to admit defeat. "I cannot break her will. Her God is more powerful."

Cyprian was disappointed. "I have been your follower because I thought you were the most powerful force, now you say there is one more powerful. Now I will follow her God."

He left all his Earthly possessions and entered a monastery where he became a pious monk. Years later, so the story goes, while preaching to infidels in Muslims countries, Cyprian and Justina were tortured and burned at the stake."

His writings and notes on sorcery were compiled into what became The Great Book of Saint Cyprian."

"And that's the book that was stolen."

"Exactly."

"Whoever has the book, killed the bookstore clerk."

"How can you tell?"

"That symbol outside the circle refers to the black goat prayer. That prayer is only found in Saint Cyprian's book and not in The Necronomicon."

"You think Julius your assistant..." Dennis was thinking hard. "Maybe we should call the police."

"No, we are going to be implicated as prime suspects."

"Look I don't have anything to do with it. How can you imply..." The wind chimes rattled as the front door opened.

"Please come in. How can I help you gentlemen?" Derazahl Al Udba said in a subservient tone.

A heavy set man, followed by a younger and skinny assistant, flashed a badge and said. "We are from the crime division and we'd like to speak with Mr. Al Udba."

The Antique Dealer was taken aback momentarily, but regaining his composure he said with a nervous laugh. "Well, that would be me." He smoothed his beard twice.

"Do you know Julius Darley, Mr. Al Udba?"

"No, I mean yes...but."

"Is that a yes or no, Mr. Al Udba? The younger assistant had pulled out a small notebook and was busy scribbling.

"Yes. He was an employee of mine."

"Was?"

"He quit two weeks ago without an explanation." He hesitated to reveal the stolen book.

"Did you have any disagreement, argument?"

"No, we didn't."

"And you haven't seen him since."

"No, but why are you asking me all this?"

"He's dead Mr. Al Udba, his body was found early this morning, or whatever was left of his body."

"How, where?" Derazahl Al Udba was clearly shaken. "What do you mean left of his body?"

"We will know more after the autopsy, but his body was dismembered and scattered through a large wooded area."

Derazahl Al Udba exchanged a knowing look with Dennis who had been following intently all this time.

"Do you know if he had any enemies? Or if he was involved in gang related activities, drugs...?"

"No, not that I know."

The heavy set detective pulled a small, clear Ziploc bag from his pocket and laid it on the table. "Do you recognize this?"

The antique Dealer held the bag up to the dim light. Inside there was a piece of yellow paper with a number of several digits written as if in a hurry, but that he did not recognize. He turned it and on the other side there were three words that again meant nothing to him.

"We found it in his pocket. Anything related to a work of art or antique Mr. Al Udba?"

"No." He read the words again but drew a blank, the number did not ring a bell either. It didn't look like a phone number, too many digits. Even if one assumed the area code was included, it was an unfamiliar one.

"Sorry, I have no idea what it is."

The detective put the bag back in his pocket and pulled out a business card. "We appreciate your cooperation; if you remember anything that may help us in the investigation, please give us a call." They turned and disappeared into the street traffic.

"What the hell is happening?" Dennis exploded "Do you notice the same M.O.? Whoever killed the kid from the bookstore also killed your assistant."

"There must be a connection."

"Maybe they knew each other, you know during lunch break."

"I know Mrs. Rothschild from the bookstore." Derazahal Al Udba said motioning Dennis to the door. "Maybe she can tell us."

They crossed the square and soon were inside the bookstore. Dennis tried his best to hide behind the shelves, ashamed of his earlier outburst at the young lady behind the counter. He waited until she hung up the intercom and signaled Derazahl Al Udba to proceed to the main office.

The office was in complete disarray, books piled up on her desk and chairs, two cardboard boxes on the floor were overflowing with more books. Mrs. Rothschild head materialized behind the desk. "Can you...?" She motioned for Derazahl and Dennis to clear the chairs and sit down. "What can I do for you gentlemen?" She was arranging some printed sheets.

"Sorry to bother you Mrs. Rothschild" Derazahl Al Udba started. "Our visit has to do with the death of your employee a week ago..."

"I'm afraid I don't have any more information..." She was looking at Dennis, "are you with the police?"

"No, name's Dennis, I am a teacher and Mr. Al Udba's acquaintance." They shook hands.

Derazahl Al Udba related the police visit and the gruesome death of his ex- employee.

Mrs. Rothschild was shaken. "Poor Julius, he used to come here all the time."

"Because the similarities of their deaths, we think they may be related in some way. Do you recall anything in particular?" Dennis piped in.

A chart on the wall had caught Derazahl Al Udba's attention. It was a training guide on how to decipher the numbers and dates of a published book and their significance.

"That's it!" Derazahl Al Udba exclaimed.

Dennis and Mrs. Rothschild turned in unison.

"It wasn't a phone number! It was the ISBN number of a book!" Derazahl Al Udba was excited.

"What are you talking about?"

"The number on the piece of paper the police found in Julius pocket."

Mrs. Rothschild's eyes were wide open. "Do you remember the number?"

He shook his head.

"But I remember the words, now that I think of it; it may be its title."

"What was it?"

"The Einstein Project."

Dennis' jaw dropped. Mrs. Rothschild dove to the keyboard to Google the name.

"Twenty two million results in point fourteen seconds." She said almost to herself. "Filtering data to books" She typed some more, "thirteen million results, oh my, even a play called The Einstein Project" she hit advanced search. "I'm going to cross reference..."

"Don't bother" Dennis' palms were upfront. "It is NOT a book and it won't be on the Web."

Mrs. Rothschild and Derazahl Al Udba turned their surprised faces. "What? You knew about this?" Derazahl Al Udba beard was shaking.

Dennis was already regretting it. "It may not be related, after all there are so many things called The Einstein Project."

"How about the ones you know about it." Mrs. Rothschild piped in.

Dennis passed his folded handkerchief over his perspiring forehead. "A scientist, friend of mine, is working on a top secret project called precisely that."

"And you don't know if your scientist friend knew Julius?"

"No, now I'm worried about him I've been trying to contact him for the last week but no luck."

"So, what do we do now? Call the police and tell them what we know?" Derazahl wondered.

"We know nothing so far." Dennis said "but you can call and ask them for the number, make something up."

The detectives reluctantly gave him the number. "We'd rather give it to you in person Mr. Al Udba, but we are making an exception only this time."

"Yes, I appreciate it, like I said I may have found a reference to that number on shipping orders...yes I'll let you know."

Mrs. Rothschild was already entering the number in the ISBN database. Almost immediately the screen displayed the title, author, publisher, etc. and on a separate window the picture of the book.

"There you have it." Mrs. Rothschild swung the monitor to face the front desk.

Again Dennis eyes went wide open. "The Necronomicon!" Derazahl made the sign of the cross.

For a few seconds Dennis was transfixed on the monitor then as if possessed, dug into his briefcase and pulled HIS Necronomicon book and checked its ISBN number against the one on the monitor display.

"It's my book; it is the number of my book!" Dennis was stunned.

"Where did you get your book from?" Mrs. Rothschild was curious.

"Right here from your bookstore, two weeks ago."

"Can't be, we don't carry anything related to the occult, witchcraft, or sorcery."

"Well, the teenager boy was at the register."

"Where exactly did you find the book?" Now Mrs. Rothschild was really mystified.

"The other assistant found it for me."

"What did he look like?"

"Older, well dressed, sideburns and a walking cane"

"You are describing Julius, Mr. Al Udba's assistant." She exchanged looks with Mr. Al Udba.

"Exactly."

"Can someone explain to me what the hell is going on?" The voice was that of Mrs. Rothschild but it was on everyone's mind.

The discussion lasted another hour without getting anywhere. They left Mrs. Rothschild and continued across the square. Dennis knew that a key piece to solving the mystery was to find The Great Book of Saint Cyprian, the stolen book.

"Yes, I totally agree with you," Derazahl said. "All we have to do is follow the trail of dead bodies."

They came to an empty bench and stopped to rest briefly. "The Book is extremely dangerous, Mr. Miller. The Monks that kept it for centuries had it chained to the wall and according to legend whoever possesses the book dies under mysterious circumstances."

"Well, obviously the teenager and your assistant came in contact with it, but so did you." Dennis waited for the reaction.

"Are you accusing me of something?"

"You have done something, haven't you?" Dennis grabbed the antique dealer by the collar and held him up off the floor. "Offering human sacrifices? How much for their souls? Huh? You tried to fool me pretending the book was stolen, didn't you?"

"No, no, please, it's not me" he was flapping his hands and gasping for air.

"Maybe I should call the police and tell them a few things, huh?"

He was pleading. "No, no I'll tell you the secret..."

Dennis set him down and straightened the antique dealer's collar and turban. "Okay, I'm all ears."

"The first page of the book warns you to proceed at your own risk and peril. Should you turn the page, your soul will forever be damned and belong to the Angel of Darkness. The secret is on the last page of the book. It is a ritual that forces the Devil to release your soul. Only a few know this and even fewer had the fortune to get to the last page." His bony hands were leafing through imaginary pages.

"And you want me to believe all this mumbo jumbo?"

"No, because you already do," the antique dealer's eyes were shining in the dark.

Dennis returned home and tried to concentrate on his everyday chores, grading exams and prepare lectures, he had upcoming finals to give but, as usual he would recycle his exams, the one from four years ago would do it.

His cell phone rang.

"Richard? Where the hell have you been...?"

"I've been working on the project and I have fantastic news! We are about to run the real experiment, not just a simulation, and I want you to witness it. I obtained clearance for you to be present. It's going to be tonight at midnight, you can't miss it" He sounded very excited.

Dennis was surprised by the rapid development. "I thought the actual experiments were years away."

"I can't say much over the phone but when you get here I'll explain, also I have to make sure you're coming to make the necessary arrangements."

"I'll try to make it..."

"No, either you are or you aren't."

"Okay, fine I'll be there."

It was an unusual request but he was curious and excited to be part of such a ground breaking experiment. Maybe this time he would learn all the details. Richard had been very secretive and had only related in general terms the purpose and objective of his research.

Dennis drove his Volkswagen Beetle, at night, traffic was light and he arrived at the University Campus with plenty of time to spare. He made a wide turn to a side entrance where a sign on a three story building read "E-139 Albert Einstein Hall - Research Laboratory"

He knocked on the metal door; the building seemed to be deserted except for a single light that shone through the window on the second floor. Three cars were parked in front of the building and had orange stickers on the lower left windshield that read "staff". The adjacent student parking lots were largely empty under the cold mercury-vapor lights.

Dennis pulled out his cell phone and clicked the highlighted number under the name Rich. "I'm downstairs" he said after the "Hello" from the other side.

"I'm coming down." Richard sounded agitated.

Dennis was taken aback by the stillness of the place, granted, he didn't expect a crowd or TV coverage, in fact he didn't know what to expect but this wasn't it.

Richard opened the door, he was wearing a black robe and a golden medallion hung from his neck.

Dennis found it a little silly, but Richard had been known as a prankster during his student days and a little bit on the rebellious side, so he wasn't surprised if this was just another way to show a little disrespect for the venerable institution.

"I'm glad you are early so I can give you the ten cent tour." He led Dennis through a set of huge sliding doors marked with the red Biohazard symbol.

"Where are the other scientists?" Dennis found himself in a semi dark cave-like chamber illuminated only by the indirect light coming from the monitors, screen displays, readouts and LED indicators. A low intensity set of Tivoli lights marked the zigzagging path through exotic machines humming softly.

"They're getting ready to get this thing going." His voice echoed from the high walls. "This is the outer perimeter of the lab, designated Biosafety Level One, where standard research is carried out on viruses not known, to cause disease in healthy adult humans, but we just call it P1."

They had reached the opposite wall where above a rotating Plexiglas door a sign read "BSL-2". Richard retrieved latex gloves and a respirator, after Dennis had done the same Richard punched a code on the alphanumeric keypad on the wall and motioned Dennis to go in.

"This is P2 where research is done on viruses with moderate potential hazard to humans, such as hepatitis A, B, and C, influenza A, and others like MRSA, and VRSA." Dennis pointed to the various machines.

Cubicles and stainless steel desks with microscopes, centrifuges and other machines populated the Lab.

"I didn't know your project involved viruses or Biohazards." Dennis said through his respirator.

"It is both. A hybrid of sorts, part high nuclear physics and advanced chemical reactions, you'll see it." He pointed to a circular stairway that led to a tower. "Follow me."

They came to a door with a band of yellow and black stripes that read "Restricted Access" and next to it, built in the wall a retractable eye reader labeled "Retinal ID" An alphanumeric keypad was hanging by scorched wires from the wall and the door was open. Inside there was a large circular room with dozens of monitors and control switches, illuminated push buttons, computer readouts and LED indicators.

"What happened here?" Dennis did not like this at all.

"This is the Isolation Control Tower." He closed the door, removed his respirator and signaled Dennis to do the same. "We had a little incident earlier today but nothing to worry about it."

Dennis noticed some monitors were flashing "BREACH! BREACH!" in red letters. That's when he realized that all indicators were alarms and high alerts; there were many rotating flashing red lights but no audio.

Richard pointed to a bank of monitors labeled "BSL-4". He selected a top view monitor of the interior and zoomed in. Dennis knew that Biosafety level four was the most toxic of all levels where the most lethal and deadliest viruses such as Marburg and Ebola are kept and for which there is NO vaccine or known cure. Two hyperbaric chambers lay in the center of the room next to two discarded Hazmat suits. The chambers were arranged to form a "T" and they were connected to various valves, hoses, pipes, cables and connectors of all kinds. Now he zoomed in to the face plate, inside, the contorted face of a scientist still alive was screaming to a muted camera.

"What's happening? Richard? What are you doing?" Dennis was now sure there was something totally wrong with this picture.

Richard did not answer right away; he focused and zoomed in on the next chamber. A comatose but still alive scientist was muttering something.

"Sublimation, Dennis!" His eyes were wide open with excitement, "the old Alchemists were right Dennis, and they were on the right track. They just didn't have the right tools to do it." He was smiling. "When you skip a phase transition, much like dry ice going from solid to gas, skipping the liquid state, wonderful things happen. Obviously I only need their brains, according to your calculations."

"You are experimenting with humans, the project I helped you with did not mention..."

"You're right but I discovered a secret, the right formula..." He pulled a black and ancient book from a drawer; the brittle leather cover seemed to have some symbols carved or impressed but vaguely visible. Attached to the cover edge were metal clasps that locked the book closed.

Dennis new what it was.

The original Necronomicon.

Richard unlatched the first clasp.

"No Richard, please don't." He lunged forward to stop him.

Richard managed to duck and hit Dennis on the ribs; the book skidded off the counter and hit the floor. The still closed clasp popped open on impact. Dennis thrashed to the floor, his face just inches from where the book came to rest. The book came open to the first page, his eyes were frozen to the last line of the curse. "...should you continue on to page two, your soul shall be forever the sole possession of the Lord of Darkness ..."

Dennis tried to reach the book. Richard was turning machines on to start the experiment. The vibration angled the book just out of his fingers' reach and the page started to turn.

Dennis looked behind him and saw Richard had entered a Kabbalistic circle raising his medallion and invoking Satan, Lord of Darkness. The Hyperbaric chambers down below were glowing in a green halo. He turned back to the book.

Page two was square in his face.

He stretched his arm all he could and managed to pick it up through the cranny, he immediately skipped to the last page. It was missing, torn out of the book.

"Are you looking for this?" Richard was holding the torn page from the book in one hand and a torch in the other.

Dennis lunged towards Richard with all his might, the handrail gave way and both flew into the firewall of plasma down below. The single page fluttered in the air for a few seconds before it was consumed by tongues of fire.

A huge explosion shook the University Campus, debris flew in all directions.

The following day the forensic team had found no survivors, no human remains. According to University records, three scientists were missing and as for the cause of the fire it was attributed to an electrical malfunction. A spokesperson from the University stated that no known projects or experiments were conducted or planned at that time and that BSL-3 and BSL-4 did not house any lethal specimens at that time.

The wind chime rattled alerting the antique dealer of a new costumer. He raised his gaze from the magnifying glass and the old papyrus. "Please come in, how can I help you?"

A young man with wire rimmed glasses and a school backpack slung on one shoulder approached the counter. "I was wondering if you are interested in buying an antique item." He said timidly as he pulled a blackened and semi-burnt book with metal clasps. "I'm sure is worth something because is very old."

"Ah, a book," the antique dealer's eyes widened but almost immediately caught himself and after only a cursory inspection he said. "Well the book is worthless but I'll give you fifty dollars for it."

"I'll take it." The student said.

As soon as the student disappeared through the door Derazahl Al Udba embraced the book holding it to his chest. "Welcome back my child." He ran down the hallway to the swinging wall laughing and hugging it.

The Samurai let out a scream.

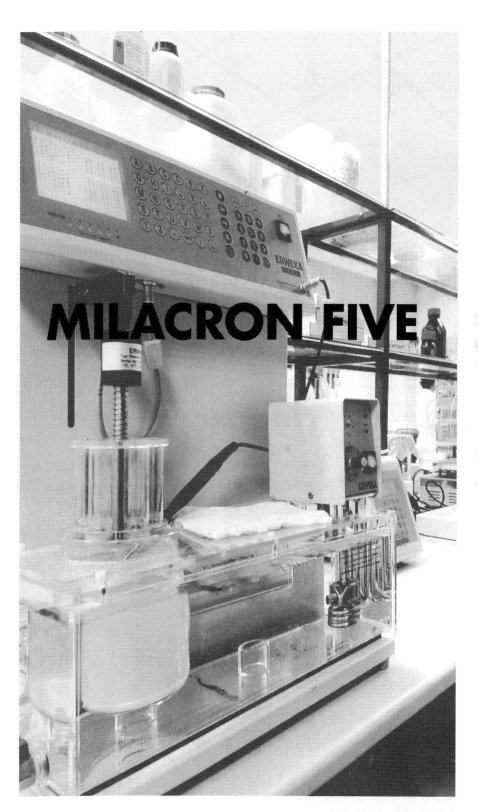

MILACRON FIVE

The banging on the door woke me up. "Open up you bastard!" I did not recognize the man's voice. But I immediately knew who the woman was. "No, please! Don't..." She was pleading and crying.

"Come on! Tell your boyfriend to come out or else!" the man's voice screamed.

"Please John, no..."

Her head smashed on the door with a sick thud.

I looked around; I was still at the Motel. The banging on the door and the wailing continued but now he was kicking the door so hard, I thought the door would fly off the hinges.

I was trying hard to make sense of what was happening. "What the hell was Lisa doing here?" Any lingering sleep had evaporated in a flash and I was fully awake now. I looked at my watch while putting on my shirt, pants and shoes almost at the same time. It was 6:47 in the morning. She had left only thirty minutes ago, so she would be home by the usual time as she did when coming from work. I raced to the bathroom searching for a rear window, no such luck.

"Come on out you son of a bitch. I know you're in there!"

Now I was sure. This was Lisa's husband, John, a burly gorilla over six feet tall.

I smelled trouble.

The screaming and banging stopped briefly and I heard Lisa's cries move away from the door and to the parking lot. "Maybe they're leaving." I sighed.

By the edge of the curtain I saw him drag Lisa into his pickup truck. He then made a u turn and stopped right in front of my room. The headlight beams pierced through the falling snow and flooded the front door and window.

Now I was trapped like a rat.

"You're going to come out sooner or later, bastard, and I'll be waiting for you!" He yelled from the semi open door of his truck, slammed it shut and waited inside.

I lifted the phone and pressed whatever it was labeled there, front desk, service, info, 911, nothing. The phone was dead. In small letters on the cradle it read "no outside calls" I was getting what I had paid for. My chest was pounding and I was running out of options.

Now I was regretting the day I told Lisa how pretty she was. Not that I lied, mind you, many men, I am sure, would have immediately agreed with me because she was a head turner. That's all I needed. I obviously, didn't care if she was married. Her excuse was that she was unhappy, perhaps like most women after ten or more years of marriage, and unlike men that use the same excuse a lot sooner.

"John, my husband," she said, "Is abusive, domineering and violent."

My reaction was. "Why don't you leave him?"

Without hesitation she added. "Because he will find me and kill me."

At that moment, any sane person in my shoes would have suddenly remembered important business to attend in Timbuktu or Siberia and fled the scene.

Not me, deep in the recesses of my mind she was the princess in distress that needed to be saved. That she was six or eight years older than I was did not matter. In fact, it gave me a sense of security that she knew what she was doing.

She was one of the hundred or so machine operators in white coats that tended the high speed assembly machines at the Company we worked for. Some operators rotated positions often, but others just stayed with a single machine for a long time. Lisa fell into that second group and had stayed with injection molding machine Cincinnati-Milacron # 5 for the last two years.

The Company manufactured electronic devices that required high precision and this was accomplished by sophisticated robotic assembly machines. Beyond the Injection Molding machines, on a separate building, there existed a Clean Room Environment where hair nets, dust masks, gloves, overshoes, and Tyvek suits were standard attire to protect the electronic components from human contamination.

Production was a non-stop process that ran 24/7. Unlike other companies that maintained a first, second and third shift to cover around the clock operation, ours was a bizarre schedule called "Four by Four" that in general terms meant four days on, four days off.

This required four shifts, namely; A, B, C, and D and worked as follows.

Shift "A" worked twelve hours, from 6 A.M. to 6 P.M. Shift "B" worked from 6 P.M. to 6 A.M. Both shifts worked for four days. Then they were off. Shifts "C" and "D" came in did the same thing and the cycle repeated. Each worker ended up working exactly 40 hours a week and still, was off four days a week.

I had chosen to work night shift, not only because it allowed me to attend college during the day, but also because it paid slightly more than day shift.

It must have been my second or third week on the job when Robert, my supervisor, called on the radio one day and said. "Gino, go and see what's wrong with Final One."

Final One was one of fifty assembly machines lined up in rows of four. Above, conveyors carrying plastic components and electronic parts moved in all directions, forming a large web of intertwined steel. The robotic assembly lines, including Final One, were fed at a dizzying speed by this continuous flow controlled by dedicated computer systems.

"We are going to need the Hi-C." I called back on the radio. "Station nine rejecting 39%." The Hi-C was a rolling/portable high speed camera with a monitor built in that could take up to 300 frames per second of high resolution video. Then replay in slow motion the superfast action of robotic arms placing or misplacing the assembled parts.

"Ten four, before you get the Hi-C check the molding that sends nine, what's nine?"

"Hubs, I think they're coming from Milacron five, I'll go check."

"Ten four."

She was sitting at a stainless steel table. Above, a sign in red letters read. "QUALITY CONTROL." Next to her, stood stacks of trays full of plastic parts that she was supposed to feed into a desktop machine with displays and readouts. Random monitoring ensured minimum or zero rejects at the final machine. She was busy applying pink nail-polish. A lock of red hair had burst from her net cover obscuring the name on the lapel of her coat.

"Excuse me miss... QC"

"Yes?" she said without looking up.

"We have hub rejects at Final One."

"No, you don't." Now she looked up. She was chewing gum. She saw I was one of the new techs.

She continued the manicure and the chewing.

"Please Miss whatever your name is, can you check these?" I had scooped a handful of parts coming out of her machine.

"I'll tell you what," she said as she moved to one side. "Why don't you check them yourself."

As an Engineering Tech responsible to maintain and run all kinds of equipment, we had been trained to test and check countless components in dozens of machines.

I fired seven tests in no time, all green, the eighth was red. I switched the monitor on and got a specific code. Switched channels on my radio to call Molding Tech Department and initiated a shut-down sequence for Milacron Five.

"Wait, you can't just come in and shut my machine down."

"Sorry Ma'am I have bad parts."

"I am calling your supervisor." She was waving the phone.

"Go ahead, and I'll call yours." I was pointing to main offices.

"Oh yeah? What are you going to tell my boss, huh?"

"Maybe he will be interested in the one thousand rejects I have on Final One, all coming from this machine, and he may casually notice your manicure, anything else Miss QC?"

I was looking at her right in the eyes.

"Yes. Are you married?

Like they say, the rest is history. We were careful to maintain our relationship under wraps for several months. Our night shift schedules rarely coincided, so, she came up with a plan where we took alternate days off every other week, so she could pretend to go to work as usual. I would wait for her at a prearranged location. From there we ended up in any of the cheap motels that dotted the area, which was the best I could afford as a college student.

The headlights flooding the front door and window of the room I was in, left me no way to escape. It must have been only a few minutes that I sat there pondering my fate, but to me, it seemed like it went on forever.

Suddenly the lights went out.

Maybe he had turned the headlights off to lure me out.

I knew it was foolish but I had no choice, I had to look. I slowly cracked the edge of the curtain. The snow was still falling but traces of daylight illuminated the parking lot.

The pickup was gone.

Maybe he had moved to the side, where I could not see him. I had to think fast, do something fast or both.

I sprang out of the room as fast as I could. Sprinted for my car, keys in hand, but the door lock in my car was semi frozen and the key would not turn. In the twilight of dawn the shadows seemed to morph and the pickup seemed to be here and there. I kept jiggling the key until it finally opened. I got inside and locked the door, still expecting to see the guy any second. I didn't feel the cold.

I turned the key on the ignition. The engine turned a few times and died. I kept trying and I could hear the starter engaging, grinding. I was pumping gas, but at the same time I did not want to flood the engine. Agonizing minutes went by. Finally it caught, and I came out skidding out of the parking lot.

I went home but parked about a block away from my apartment to discover and drop anyone tailing me.

No one had.

Tired as I was, I still had to go to my classes at U of I but it was hard to concentrate on anything. What the hell had happened? How did he find out? How did he find me at the hotel?

This week I still had two more days off from work, which I used to cool down a little. I could not break one of the rules of the game; call her home. Not that it mattered anymore. Well, maybe now more than ever I should keep quiet or else risk her life. So, I did not make any attempts to call her.

Three days later when I returned to work. She wasn't there. A friend of hers told me Lisa was going to be off the entire week.

The following night, at work, started just like any other night. At around three o'clock in the morning, right after our last break, Robert, My supervisor called me to his office.

"There is a message for you Gino." He said reading a sticky note. "His name is John and he said he is coming to pick you up at six o'clock in the morning." He paused. "He said you know about it."

My face must have turned white, because then he asked. "Is everything all right? Are you OK?"

"Yeah, everything is fine, car problems, but nothing serious." I was trying to keep a poker face but it wasn't working.

"Thanks Robert" I said trying to sound casual and exited the office.

I knew a number of Johns, but only one could be heading this way. Lisa's husband.

I needed to clear my head. I went to the bathroom and splashed cold water on my face.

"Six o'clock!" I said to the mirror in desperation.

"Whaaat?" a sleepy voice from the last stall whispered. "I told you to wake me up earlier!"

I tiptoed out.

What the hell was I going to do? Leave the job and never come back? I had to think of something, and I didn't have much time. Come to think of it, this was the only place he could find me. He didn't know where I lived, nor did Lisa. I had to figure out something for the long run, but for now I wasn't going to wait.

I went to my supervisor's office.

"Hey, Robert" I said nonchalant. "I have to leave early today at five o'clock, if you don't have any inconvenience."

"Oh, the a…" He hesitated trying to recall either the message or the car problem.

"Yeah, yeah" I cut in before he could actually think about it.

"No problem," he said, returning to his papers. "Just get your paperwork ready before you leave."

At five o five I was sneaking out of the parking lot through a back gate with my lights out and breaking to a minimum.

The following day I took my second car to work. John did not know this car. This time I parked on the adjacent parking lot we shared with the company next door. I could not ask to leave early this time but at regular quitting time I left through the back door.

Later that day after returning from school the phone rang. Finally Lisa was calling.

"THIS IS JOHN" the commanding voice on the other side of the line said.

I froze. How did he get my phone number?

I thought about slamming the phone, or say it was wrong number, but finally I thought; what the hell, let him talk. But I still didn't know what to say.

"I SAID THIS IS JOHN," he repeated.

He sounded mad. That he was harmless on the phone gave me just enough strength to stay on the line. But his voice had an edge of cockiness and arrogance.

Just before I said, "SO?" he said.

"You son of a bitch! You think you're too smart, huh?"

"Listen, I..."

"Huh? Now you can talk. Look bastard, for the last four days you managed to sneak out like a rat and I'm getting tired of your little game. But I AM GONNA GET YOU" Now he was screaming, yelling and cursing.

"Look I..." In my mind I replayed the many times I had told Lisa how stupid the idea of cheating on her husband was, she had smiled and said. "Is only bad if he finds out about us, but I won't tell him. Would you?" and we both had laughed.

"DO YOU UNDERSTAND ME?" He was getting louder and I could hear glass breaking in the background, more cursing, more swearing. Again I wanted to hang up but, fighting the urge I figured, what the hell, he might have a point.

"DO YOU UNDERSTAND ME?" He repeated.

What the hell did he want me to understand? By now with all that shouting I didn't know what the question was. I thought. "OK pal, I understand everything you say I am. Also, I understand that you are going to kill me. I totally agree with you, no hard feelings." But I did not want to upset him more than he already was.

"Yeah, Yeah... What do you... want?" I finally managed to say.

"WHAT DO I WANT?" this was followed by more swearing. "I WANT YOU TO LEAVE MY WIFE ALONE."

This surprised me and at the same time made me feel a great sense of relief. "How come you didn't say that before?" I thought. At least I knew she was still alive. My next thought was. "You mean you don't want to kill me anymore?" This was so freaking good!

"I DON'T WANT YOU TO TALK TO MY WIFE, I DON'T WANT YOU TO SEE HER ANYMORE AND I DON'T WANT YOU TO EVEN THINK ABOUT HER. IS THAT CLEAR TO YOU?"

"Yes, I understand loud and clear..."

"If I find out that you keep molesting her, then you know what's going to happen to you, don't you?"

I had to bite my tongue to take the last insult because this wasn't fair. One thing was to be the guy screwing his wife and I could take all the insults for that. Hey, I had even started to feel sorry for the guy at one point. But, molesting her?

"I want you to say it, so you get it." He ordered.

"OK, I promise I won't talk to her anymore. I will not see her, I will not think about her, and I will not..." I suddenly realized I was talking to a dead phone.

I did not see her until the following week when she was back to work. I had to talk to her and find out what had happened.

Her face bore the fading marks of cuts and bruises. "Are you okay?" I felt guilty.

"Yeah, I'm fine." She smiled.

"I'm really sorry..." I started.

"No." She cut in. "It wasn't your fault! It was nobody's fault." She looked away and her voice faltered, "Just the story of my life." She said trying to hold her tears.

She looked fragile. "What happened that day after you left the hotel?"

"He was waiting for me in front of the house. He knew I wasn't coming from work."

"How...?"

"He called me at work to ask me for something. When my supervisor told him I had taken the day off, he suspected something was up and started looking for my car in all the motels in the area. When he didn't find it, he just waited for me at home. He wouldn't even let me explain. He just started hitting me really hard and he said he was going to kill me if I did not tell him the truth. So, I had to. He dragged me to the motel and I had to tell him what room you were in." She wiped rolling tears. "I'm sorry but I had no choice."

I couldn't blame her. "Don't worry, that's okay. But then he drove away. Why?"

"Well, before that, he parked his pick up in front of your room. He was going to wait there until you got out, then kill you. That's when he realized he had left the gun at the house so we drove back, got the gun and hailed back to the motel. He wouldn't leave me at home because he wanted me to witness your death. The round trip didn't take more than twenty minutes. But, by the time we got back your car was gone." She sobbed.

My mind went numb and my legs felt rubbery. To learn that I had escaped by mere seconds by his bad memory. That was shocking. I was speechless.

"He beat me up so bad." She continued. "That he had to take me to the hospital." She removed her hairnet and showed me the stitches on the back of her head. I could still see the dried blood. "He made up the story that I had been robbed and beaten up by two Gangbangers." Her tears had dried out now. "You see all I have to go through? I hate him, I hate him so much."

I didn't know what to think anymore. I didn't even know what she wanted. But I knew exactly what I had to do.

"I think it is a good idea if we just stop seeing each other. What do you think?"

"You don't want to be with me anymore?" Her eyes were dreamy and her voice huskier and we were starting to draw stares from nosey coworkers.

"I fear for your safety." I lied. "I think we can cool it off for a while."

"Okay, just for a while." She said with a wicked smile.

I walked away shaking my head "for a while?" I was done. As hard as it was to say no I realized I had been given a second chance. I was living on borrowed lives. I didn't want anything to do with her. "Why is it that some people never learn?"

From then on I tried to avoid Milacron Five like the plague. For the next two weeks everything was quiet then the phone calls started again. "Hey, how come you haven't stopped by my machine? I called you yesterday but you were not home." Then the hand-written notes, "don't you want to talk to me anymore? I didn't do anything to you. We can still see each other like before."

"You are absolutely crazy!" I told her when I did finally stop by her machine. "We are NOT supposed to see each other, remember?"

"Yeah, but this time I have a better plan." She winked. "He'll never find out."

"No, no. He is going to beat you up again, or worse kill you!" Now I was beginning to doubt her sanity.

"I'm telling you I have everything figured out. All we got to do is..."

"Stop! Stop! I don't want to hear it." I could not believe it, after all those beatings. What was it that drove her to do this?

"Don't you love me anymore?" She started crying.

"Look, it is better if we don't see each other, ever, OK? I'm sorry. Please...don't call me." I walked away.

"Wait. . . I'm going to kill myself!"

I hesitated momentarily; in her deranged state of mind she was capable of doing it. But more likely it was just another trick up her sleeve. I had to summon all my will not to turn back.

I kept walking.

A few weeks later I could not help to notice that a molding technician was spending long stretches of time talking to her and sometimes leaving the premises together. It was her life and she could do whatever she wanted with it. More than jealousy I was concerned and terrified of what was going to happen next. "What if the husband thinks it is still me!"

I hoped her new plan worked this time.

More than a month passed without incident until one day I noticed she wasn't there anymore. Someone else was tending Milacron Five. "Maybe she took days off or maybe she was on vacation." I said to myself. But the weeks passed and she still did not show up.

"She quit about a month ago." A lady said when I casually asked around. "I am still mad at her because she did not tell us anything. Her husband came to pick up her stuff from her locker about three weeks ago. I think they were moving back to North Carolina." she rolled her eyes. "I don't understand her".

Now I realized that I hadn't seen the molding tech either, maybe he was there, there were so many technicians that you just didn't notice.

"He is no longer with the Company." Another molding tech told me later. "But, I don't know why. He didn't talk a lot, you know."

Maybe, now he was talking a lot less.

Did he receive a message? "John will pick you up at six o'clock in the morning." Or, perhaps, John had wised up and hadn't called at all.

**OVER HER
DEAD BODY**

The wailing of the approaching ambulance woke me up from deep sleep. The siren stopped around the corner. Almost immediately the red flashing lights hit my window and moved two houses down on the other side of the street by old Mrs. Marin's house.

"I guess she's sick again." I said with a tad of uneasiness. "But, why do they have to wake up the entire neighborhood?"

The red LEDs on my alarm clock read 4:15 AM. I was going to be lucky if I got two more hours of sleep. Just as I was tucking myself back in bed, more flashing lights arrived and now I could hear voices from her driveway. Mrs. Marin was crying and pleading in a sense of urgency.

So much for a quiet rest.

From my driveway I could see under the blue and red flashers the paramedics rolling down a loaded gurney into the back of the ambulance. "Please save him! Please Robert don't die." Mrs. Marin was clenching her bony hands to the side rails of the gurney.

"He'll be fine lady." A man in a blue uniform was saying, trying to hold her back, but then relenting and helping her ailing body up to join her son.

Al, the other son, stood there watching alone in the driveway. He watched the ambulance close its doors and speed away. He was smoking his cigar, with his grey hair clearly visible under the dim porch light. Soon the rest of the patrol vehicles and firefighter trucks left.

I crossed the dark street. "Hey! Al, what happened?" I said as a way of greeting.

"Robert and his drugs," he said sucking on the last remains of a stinking cigar. "I guess he can't have enough."

"You mean..."

"Yeah." He spat on the flower pot by the entrance way, stepped on the cigar stub and killed it with a rolling motion. "Good night," he said before disappearing inside the house.

Al was not much of a talker; in fact he talked very little. But the few words that he and I had exchanged in the past did not indicate any mental disorder. Maybe he was a little awkward and socially shy, but that did not stop him from riding his bicycle everyday to a family restaurant a few blocks away where he worked as a dishwasher, a job that he had held for years. That in itself spoke volumes to attest to his near wellbeing and normalcy.

"He is not in his right mind!" Mrs. Marin would often say, then in a whisper. "My poor baby is mentally retarded." She would add when Allen was not around.

"Robert is the smart one, he can do anything." She would say with pride, but oblivious to the fact that Robert would not or could not keep a job. "I work whenever they call me." He often said, I never did figure out who "they" were. But I often saw him riding his bicycle to the grocery store nearby where he would hang out with other unsavory characters.

Often times he would disappear for months at a time. "He went to visit his cousin in New York." Mrs. Marin explained, masking the fact that he was a guest at the local jail, compliments of the justice department.

"Can you mow the lawn and trim the bushes for me?" She would ask me now and then. At first I gladly did it, but when years passed and the asking turned into a habit I suggested maybe Robert or Al could do it.

"No, they don't know because, well, they were born in New York, you know." She said matter of fact.

One day I learned that, to her long list of ailments, she just had added the more fashionable Alzheimer's disease. I found this out the hard way. One day a handyman came to do some repairs to her house. She was short ten dollars. You can imagine where she got the ten dollars from. Anyway, "I'll pay you next week." She told me. A week turned into two, then three. When I finally got the courage to remind her of her debt, she flew into a rage and threatened to call the cops on me for trying to scheme ten dollars out of a poor old lady. She said that I was not nice and that she would never talk to me again. To prove that indeed she had the dreaded disease she was knocking on my door the following day saying that she was sorry. That she could not remember anything from the previous day, could I go fix a water leak?

I knew that Robert was an alcoholic. The usual yelling and screaming from their house was proof of that. He could not own a vehicle because his driver's license had been revoked permanently, but, drugs? Well, I wasn't surprised. Maybe that's why he had never moved away, or got married, since he had just enough to support his habit.

Robert was the oldest. Then there was his younger sister Liza, now in her mid-fifties and married to a ruthless contractor that, according to the rumor mill, had ties to the organized crime. What I did know for certain was that; despite that she lived nearby she rarely visited her mother. I wasn't surprised she didn't, the way Mrs. Marin referred to her only daughter was always in undignified terms that involved the female canine. Al, like Robert, had never married either, and both had lived with their mom in the same dilapidated house for the last thirty years since the day they moved from New York in the early eighties.

Robert never returned from the hospital. He was dead on arrival and the cause of death was from an overdose.

"Overdose of what?" I asked Mrs. Marin later.

She didn't know.

From then on Mrs. Marin's attitude turned more somber and fatalistic. The trips to the hospital became more frequent. When it was not me, playing taxicab, it would be other neighbors, social workers or church volunteers pitching in. One day the hospital trips stopped, days later I ran into her.

"I noticed you haven't been to the hospital lately, you must be feeling a lot better." I said cheering her up.

"They don't want me at the hospital anymore." For a moment I thought she was going to cry.

"Who?" I said thinking of her daughter and Al.

"The doctors, who else." She was mad. "They know I'm sick, they even found another disease, like, Hypo...something, but I'm going to find a lawyer and sue them."

I guess I really didn't know how bad she was until days later when the phone rang. "Can you come over, please?" She sounded worried. I headed her way.

"What is it Mrs. Marin?"

"That hole was not there yesterday." She was pointing to a small dirt mound next to a dug out hole in the backyard.

Nearby, her dog slept.

"The dog did it." I said right away.

"How can you blame my dog?" She was serious and annoyed. "My dog would never do something like that. This was done by somebody trying to break in." She added. "Can you fix it?"

"Yeah, no problem, I'll just put the dirt back in."

"No, no, I want you to put cement in it."

"What? Why? You don't need it." I was a little mystified.

"I want you to do it."

"Look, you don't need cement. Plus... well, we don't have any."

"No, but I'll give you the money to go buy it." She started digging in her purse.

"Mrs. Marin, you know, it is a lot of work. You have to mix it, maybe you need sand, gravel, and like I said..."

"If you don't do it I'm going to kill myself." I scrutinized her face for a hint of a joking sign, there wasn't any.

My initial thought was, "Go right ahead, make my day." I did not say anything but I started laughing at the absurdity of the threat. She just stared at me with disdain and hatred. Now I couldn't stop laughing. I was having a ball, until she said. "And I am going to make it look like you did it." Her piercing eyes seemed to slice like cold daggers.

Suddenly it wasn't funny anymore.

"What?" Now she definitely had to be kidding. "You're going to do what?"

"Just what you heard," her wrinkles were deeper and her lower lip was shivering. "You think I'm stupid. Don't you?" her bony finger shooting imaginary darts.

I had to switch tactics. Was I dealing with a psychopath? I had to be careful. Whatever I did or said could have serious consequences.

I dragged a chair and sat closer to her. "Mrs. Marin." I said in a slow and calm tone. "I wish I could help you but I am not a Mason. I don't know how to do it."

"Didn't you do your fence with cement reinforced posts?" her eyes visualizing four, five years in the past.

"Damn! Where is Mr. Alzheimer when you need him?"

Her requests became more bizarre and unusual. Next thing I knew she wanted to change every lock in her house. Then she wanted to buy a gun, and just before she fell and dislocated her knee, she was looking for a boyfriend "with good intentions." I never found out what that meant because next thing I knew she was dead.

It must have been around noon. I was sitting at my computer writing the very first story for this book, when insisting knocking on the door got my attention. An old man in paint stained dungarees was already walking away down my driveway. "Hey!" I called.

The man turned halfway still talking on his cell phone and just pointed to Mrs. Marin's house. By the time I arrived to Mrs. Marin's porch the handyman was already pocketing his cell phone and heading to his unfinished paint job next door.

"The ambulance is on its way." He said and disappeared.

Mrs. Marin was laying on the floor, but conscious, holding her knee and bawling in pain.

"What happened?"

"I tripped with the dog's leash and fell. Ouch! I think I broke my knee!"

"Look, it is important that you remember that." I said surveying the scene of the crime and mindful of contaminating or destroying potential evidence. In my mind I could see myself in the seat of the accused and a lawyer walking to the front of a jury saying something like; "Exhibit A, dog leash next to victim indicates the defendant is innocent."

"Please help me get up." She said in pain.

"Don't move!" The ambulance was bending the corner. I ran to the street to flag them down. I gave them a brief summary. Then more paramedics arrived in fire trucks, lowered a stretcher, and did a cursory check on her knee.

"You're going to be all right." One of them said, calmly. "It is nothing serious." They rolled her over the stretcher and onto the waiting ambulance. The fire trucks were already pulling away with a sense of disappointment, and then the ambulance drove slowly and quietly away.

That would be the last time I saw Mrs. Marin alive, within a week she was dead.

I stood there on Mrs. Marin's drive way. The street was empty and I had an uneasy feeling of something not being right. It was not because of Mrs. Marin's injury, I knew it was not life threatening. It was something else but I could not pin point what it was.

I had to let Al know his Mom was at the Hospital, but I did not have a phone number where to reach him. He would be back from work at five in the evening. I did not know how to reach his sister either. I recalled that during the countless times Mrs. Marin asked for assistance I suggested calling her daughter. Mrs. Marin flew into a rage and said that she'd rather die before calling her. She never forgave her daughter and son-in-law having attempted to put her in a nursing home a few years back.

"They want my house; they want to get rid of me because they also want my money and my jewelry. They will get it but over my dead body!"

So there I was, trying to think what to do next. I went over to my house, wrote a message for Al and put it on his door.

Then it hit me, I suddenly realized what was wrong. None of the paramedics ever asked me a single question. The moment they arrived I started explaining the little I knew, strangely none of them seemed to pay any attention to what I was saying.

At one point when the fire trucks with more paramedics arrived, out of the corner of my eye I caught a glance exchange between them rolling their eyes, but at that time I did not think anything of it. They never asked me if I was a relative, if she had a doctor, whether she was taking any medicine, or if a relative was coming. Now that I started thinking about it, they never mentioned what hospital they would take her to. I had just assumed it was the one I always took her to. The more I thought about it, the more strange I found it, then I recalled that almost as an afterthought before she was taken into the ambulance I had stashed her purse, hopefully with her IDs, right on the stretcher.

The following day I went to the house next door where the painter had gone into to see if I could ask him some questions. The lady of the house did not know anything about a handyman. She had not hired or contracted anybody for several months.

All these details did not take any significance at that time. I just thought it was weird. Not until a week later when Al knocked on my door and in a very casual tone said "My mom died today, just to let you know."

"What?" I could not believe it.

"I s-a-i-d t-h-a-t m-y m-o-m..."

"I'm sorry Al. I understand what you're saying. It's just...how did it happen?"

"Well, when she was bitten by the dog. She broke her leg and ..."

"Are you talking about when the ambulance took her to the hospital and I left you a message?"

"Yeah, last week," he said chomping on his cigar. For a minute I thought he was talking about a different event, what was that about being bitten by the dog? That same day I left him a message when he returned

I made sure he knew his mom was at the hospital, I asked him to call his sister. "I already did." he had said. Just two days ago I had asked him how she was doing. "She's fine." he said. Now she was dead, something was not right.

"Was she at the hospital by the lake?"

"No, she was at a nursing home."

"How did she end up in a nursing home I thought...?"

"My sister said that it was good for her."

"I thought she was at the hospital all this time..."

"No, she was at the hospital for only one day. At the nursing home they had nurses that every time my mom started yelling they would give her a shot of medicine. Then she would get better and go back to sleep."

"When your mom was yelling what did she say?"

"She wanted to come home."

"This morning when your sister was told your mom died, did she take you to the nursery home?"

"No, she came to help me clean my mom's room."

They had executed step two: The jewelry.

The funeral home was unusually crowded, mostly from members of the church Mrs. Marin had attended years before. Not that she cared much about religion, she never trusted anybody with a Bible.

"I just go to play Bingo, gossip and complain." She used to say, but the last year before her death she had stopped going to church altogether because her arthritis had made it impossible to stand or kneel for prolonged periods of time. She would sit by the front porch on an old rocking chair that had seen better days and threatened to come apart with every swing.

"My only distraction, nowadays," she would say, "is to watch people and traffic on the street." The problem was that hours would go by without a single car going by unless it was a lost drug pusher looking for the dealer around the corner.

At the funeral home, Liza was seated at the far end in the back seats, trying, unsuccessfully, to stay out of sight. You could almost hear the veiled whispers. "That's her, the daughter."

She did not speak, nor did she acknowledge visitors or accept condolences, but her husband did and in an effort to appear jovial and close to her mother-in-law he approached the podium and said. "She was good to us, we got a loan from her and we never paid it back. Ha! Ha! Ha!"

I could not believe my ears, this was the ultimate insult. I looked at the audience and there was a stoned silence. He started to say something but when some people got up and left, he relented and sheepishly went to the back seats where his wife was burying her face in her hands. He whispered something and the two left through the back door. I almost expected Mrs. Marin to jump out of the coffin and chase after the ungrateful pair.

After the rumor of disapproving comments died out Al did take the podium and thanked people for attending and coming to pay their last respects to Mrs. Marin. People filed out for a final view, and when it was my turn I thought I could see some faint footprints over her dead body.

The bastards had done it.

COUNTDOWN

T-46:22:59

A tiny hairline crack had developed deep in the massive inner wall of the electric furnace. The furnace held in its belly 44,000 pounds of molten iron that glared with a blend of golden shades, from the iridescent whites to the dark vanishing reds, and if you looked at it long enough you would see white flashes that danced on the surface.

Workers in reflective gear and dark tinted helmets approached the edge now and then, with long metal probes that inserted into the bubbly liquid. The probe melted on contact giving off a shower of bright sparks. At that point the computers and instruments in the control room would register and update the temperature, stabilizing it at 4,000 degrees Fahrenheit.

Closed loop system based on multiple factors would increase, lower or maintain the preset temperature by sending a signal to the electric contactors and starters buried deep in the tunnels under the furnaces. Thick copper bars run alongside the tunnel ceiling carrying in excess of 25,000 Amps of current to each of the ten furnaces above. A hissing sound emanated from the bus bars and the hair on one's arms danced to the whispering song.

The crack growing inside the wall of furnace number six was nothing unusual. According to engineering reports, hairline-cracks did develop after twelve weeks of continuous exposure. Hence the rigid schedule of shut-downs and revamps.

The shut-down and revamp consisted of replacing the inner wall and a complete thorough inspection of the copper coil. The copper coil was a thick pipe that looped around midway the wall more than thirty times and carried pressurized cooling fluid in its interior. The copper metal itself carried the extremely high current needed to create the intense magnetic field that melted the iron in the furnace's core.

This inner wall that protected the copper coil, was made out of two layers of high grade refractory brick, asbestos sheets, and ceramic fiber compound.

The firewall was now compromised and furnace number six was doomed.

T-39:17:42

Mark West slammed his pencil on the desk and got up with the phone still glued to his ear. He rolled his eyes again silently cursing and walked to the chart on the wall.

"...but it was supposed to be here last week!" He said cutting in the voice on the other end. "No, no, number six scheduled shut down was last week, not this week...yes we are running past the safety margin...I understand that, but...three more days, okay fine, but not a day more!" He hung up and now his head was throbbing.

"Now what's their excuse?" Assistant supervisor Tim Sutton said manning the monitors and readouts.

"The cheap bastards, the servo valves are not here yet for number one, and there is no way we can get number eight and nine back on line"

He was looking at the chart. "Management wants me to keep six up and running for three more days."

"That's insane" Tim said across the control room and twirling his finger around his temple.

I had joined the Company two years before and employment at the Foundry was extremely demanding. As an electrician in charge of maintaining the equipment and keeping systems up and running I was often privy of the issues that affected production.

"How about if we swap the servos from nine" I ventured, as I made the last connections on a new electronic control.

"I don't think it is a good idea to disturb the servos. We could end up causing more problems than the ones we already have." Mark said returning to his chair.

"How about shutting down line one, then we could even run with fifty per cent of the furnaces." Tim added.

Mark was growing more concerned. "They don't want to shut down a single line."

"I can't believe we have three furnaces out of service at the same time, it has never happened before." Tim knew it was time to worry.

"Yeah, and if we shut down number six we will be in big trouble." Mark was still eyeing the chart trying to juggle the numbers in his head.

"It's only three more days, it will be alright"

"I hope you're right Tim. Hey Gino, are you done with the new Frequency Drive?"

"Yeah, just about wrapping it up."

"Good, because here comes first shift, OK guys, Gino, Tim, give them the pass- down and lets get out of here." Mark said picking up his paperwork.

Outside the control room, heat waves rose from the long row of furnaces all the way up to the massive traversing crane. The old crane, camouflaged in soot and dust, moved silently high above by the dark roof and dropped blocks of compressed metal into the active furnaces.

T-23:55:31

The fracture had grown larger. The molten metal had wedged its way deeper through the asbestos compound and refractive brick of the inner wall. Now it was inching its way slowly. Just ahead, the copper coils loomed larger, hissing with the extreme deadly current.

The bus came to a stop under a row of mercury vapor lights. Jagged shadows from the long buildings greeted the passengers exiting at this last stop of the bus route. Trailing the long line I joined my coworkers, now lined up through the security checkpoint.

The smell was overpowering. People said you grew accustomed to it, I wasn't. After two years of working for the foundry I was sick and tired of the fumes, the heat, dust, smoke and the noise. Added to that was the extreme danger of working under falling chunks of red hot metal or burning sand from the overhead chain carrying freshly cast iron parts. Also, you had to keep an eye open at all times for moving machinery coming from the least expected places.

To traverse the vast, dark and cavernous expanses within the plant, the safest way was the catwalk, a network of steel trails high above the jungle of sparks and iron. The tradeoff was that you had to climb the long and not very safe vertical ladders.

After checking my ID, the security guard waved me in and I followed the arrow on a weather beaten sign that read; "EMPLOYEES ONLY". Another sign next to it read. "VISITORS, VENDORS AND OTHERS" and pointed in the opposite direction. I always wondered what "others" meant.

The lockers were on the second floor and although housed in the same production building they were fairly far from the furnaces. Endless rows of gray metal faced a center bench that ran the entire length and ended by the open showers on the opposite wall.

"Hey Billy Bob, wake up!" The old man sleeping on the bench and already dressed up in full gear sat up and looked at his watch. "Relax." I said zipping up my blue coveralls. "We have plenty of time."

"You always have plenty of time." He said scooping up his yellow helmet.

The circulating rumor was that Bill had started working for the company some thirty odd years ago. Because he was the best electrician he was soon promoted to supervisor. Shortly after his promotion his wife and little daughter died in a car accident. He started missing days and a bottle of wine was found in his locker. The company offered him a deal he could not refuse. He would stay with the company but back in his old position. Management figured they'd rather have an excellent electrician than a lousy supervisor.

"So, how was your weekend Billy?"

"Same old, same old, how about yours?"

"Mine? Working! Maybe one day when I am an old timer like you I'll get the weekends off. Hey! Maybe when you retire I can get your days, what is it? Two years from now?" I finished tying up my steel toe boots.

"One year, one month, and nine days." He said counting his fingers. "Then I'm out of here forever." His eyes shined envisioning some paradise.

"Wow! You're lucky." I clicked my tool belt, grabbed my helmet, respirator, safety glasses, and gloves.

"You're young, Gino." He shrugged. "Just don't make the same mistake I made." He said donning his helmet as we headed downstairs.

"What's that?"

"I stayed here too long, you have no idea how many times I wanted to just quit, escape this damned place, but there was always something. Anyways, I'm almost there."

T-23:35:09

"Alright ladies listen up!" The supervisor's voice beamed over the rumbling machinery. "It is rotation time. Tomorrow, go straight to your new assigned area." He said waving the new schedule to the twenty some electricians gathered there for the ritualistic daily pass-down.

"Today wrap up anything you have pending and I want a full report by zero seven hundred sharp. That's all, dismissed!" In his mind he was still the old drill Sergeant back in Parris Island frightening new recruits, and we did not feel any different than those poor souls did some ten years before.

"What you got, Bill?" I said catching up with him as we walked out of the electrical shop.

"Furnaces" He did not sound happy.

"God I hate the Furnaces." In fact everybody did. "I got Machining." I tried to hide my smile.

"You bastard" he punched me in the shoulder. "You want to swap?"

"No way Jose!" now I was laughing.

"Hey Billy, since you're going to Furnaces, let me give you a quick run-down. Furnace Number six was due for shutdown and revamp two weeks ago but it is still running because there are three furnaces already down and management wants the numbers. Number one is down because it needs two servo valves that hopefully will be here in five days. Once number one is up and running then number six will be shut down."

"So, what's your suggestion?"

"Rather than waiting that long I was wondering if we could swap valves with nine. In other words, cannibalize number nine, get number one up and running and shut down number six NOW. But Mark West said that it was dangerous and complicated." He looked into the distance and I could see his mind reeling.

"Not complicated," he said with his usual cool. "You just got to know what you're doing. I'll tell you more about it later." He waved as he disappeared in the direction of the Sandblasters.

Secretly I knew that Billy was sent now and then to troubleshoot the most complex problems, which was something I deeply admired. I had adopted him as my mentor and he never complained about my pesky and inquiring questions.

I headed to the furnaces section.

By the end of the shift I had studied everything related to Servo Valves from the prints and manuals. "Don't worry about it." Mark told me at one point. "Billy is going to be here tomorrow."

He did not seem too worried as he had been the day before. But the dark rings around his eyes betrayed a sleepless night. I obviously had more questions for Billy but I did not see him the rest of the day.

"Oh well, I'll ask him tomorrow" I thought as I clocked out and headed home.

T-08:12:51

Deep in the inner wall of furnace number six, the fracture had grown into a long and wide blade shape that was still growing, expanding, headed at a right angle for the deadly coils. A tongue of searing metal had breached the first refractive brick wall, pierced through layers of asbestos and now it was furiously grinding through the last line of defense. The last refractive brick wall was crumbling only inches separating both deadly forces.

T-00:01:01

The following day I arrived at work as usual. Climbed the metal stairway to the second floor and opened my locker. As I hung up my jacket I looked at the center bench.

It was empty.

Where the hell was Bill? I looked at my watch again; 10.40pm. We did not clock in until 11:00 pm but he was usually there about this time lying on the bench, "unwinding" he called it. Maybe he called in sick, I said to myself as I gathered my protective gear. Today, or rather tonight I had to report to my new assigned area.

The locker room was now crowded, doors slamming, people talking, swearing, and complaining.

T-00:00:00

The first thing I noticed was the silence.

Then somebody yelled. "It's an earthquake!"

I looked up and the fluorescent fixtures hanging from long chains up the steel structure were swinging and a thick cloud of dust was raining down. The lights flickered and a deep rumbling shook the entire building.

The lights went out.

An earsplitting explosion tore part of the wall and the bright flash froze the picture of metal crashed and screaming faces, stampeding trying to find the stairway. I flattened myself against the wall trying to make sense of what was happening. Instinctively I put on my respirator. Again, it was total darkness. My flashlight was still in my tool belt. When I turned it on, I could barely see the light beam through the dust and smoke, but nothing else.

I could hear more yelling and screaming, but could not understand any of it. By feel I found the stairway already crammed with people screaming, pushing and shoving. I was caught on the pandemonium flowing downstream. People reaching the first floor stopped in their tracks, surprised to step on hot running water, only to be crashed by the wave behind.

Red flashers were active indicating the path to the emergency exits but one could barely see them through the steaming water vapor, dust, smoke and debris. The emergency exit was blocked by a twisted metal frame. Fires were bursting everywhere, why?

"Gas! The gas lines!" Somebody yelled. Alarms were blaring through part of the building and the noise was deafening. A group of three or four of us had split from the large crowd.

"The loading area, the loading area!" I was yelling through my respirator and pointing to the escape route.

"No, No." Two of them agitatedly pointed to the flames hugging the walls and the crisscrossing steam jets from broken pipelines and bolted in the opposite direction. Rushing water strewn with debris knocked me off balance and I hit the floor. I was swept by the current for a couple feet before a strong hand pulled me by my tool belt.

"Hang on, I got you." One from the group was still with me. The running water was knee deep and climbing. From the debris I picked up a metal plate, it was a blown door locker. Using it as a shield we went through the jets of steam and bursting flames from gas lines. I had lost my flashlight and respirator. We were zigzagging our way by the light from the larger flames far ahead through collapsed walls. We came to a landing above water level and we just collapsed there coughing and sneezing. The smoke was choking us and we could not see anything. I no longer knew where we were. We were lost. We heard screams and calls for help that then vanished or stopped, we couldn't tell. Suddenly another violent explosion far ahead shook the remnants of the structure. A stairway crumbled next to us in a cloud of dust. We heard voices coming our way, then, powerful light beams pierced through the dark.

"Anybody here?"

I never thought I would be so happy to see a Firefighter. They took us to an ambulance where we were treated for smoke inhalation. The place was crowded.

More fire trucks were approaching fast, and the ones already there were deluging with foam the smoldering nearby building. More ambulances were rolling in. Half a block away, part of the massive building was blown to pieces and the entire furnace section was in flames.

Paramedics took the critically ill and injured to a nearby hospital. I was in one of the many groups that were taken to the company clinic and treated for minor cuts and bruises and sent home.

T+10:15:42

The following day I went back to find out what had happened. The entire area was cordoned off with yellow tape that read "POLICE DO NOT CROSS". No visitors, sightseers or employees were allowed. But firefighter trucks were still at the scene and several patrol vehicles guarded the perimeter where the news media had gathered with their vans and reporters. But even at this distance, the magnitude of the devastation was evident and overwhelming. Scorched and twisted metal was what remained of the entire section that had been the furnaces; smoke was still rising from the charred remains. That's when it hit me.

Bill, Billy Bones was there!

The main offices and other corporate buildings on the opposite side of the property were not affected and the company had set a relief and assist center to deal with the crisis. A large crowd had gathered.

"Are you a relative?" A lady that seemed to be holding two independent conversations on the phones finally said.

"No, but..."

"We're sorry but we cannot give you that information." She turned back to her phones.

A woman in the line behind me, seeing my frustration, tapped me on the shoulder. "Maybe you should try that." She pointed to a sign on the wall that read. "Family and relatives are advised to check with Mount Sinai Hospital..."

That was an idea.

Before heading to the hospital I tried to find out what had happened. People milling around just knew that there had been an explosion. I also gathered that Mark West and Tim Sutton had not been in the area at that time.

A welding supervisor I knew said. "I do not know any details of what happened, all we know is that it was a malfunction with one of the furnaces."

T+12:56:28

The young lady at the information desk of Mount Sinai pointed to a hallway and said. "Follow the green line. It will take you to intensive care."

At the intensive care desk there was a line of about four people, brothers, and moms, from what I heard. Then it was my turn.

"William?" The attendant said looking at a clipboard list.

"Yes, my Uncle."

"You can't see him or talk to him." she said consulting another clipboard.

"But..."

"Let me put it this way, he cannot talk to you or see you. He is in a coma, third degree burns on ninety percent of his body. He is undergoing treatment right now."

"But you can try tomorrow." She said.

T+82:16:46

"The company is on temporary shutdown, until further notice." I was told three days later when I went to pick up my last paycheck. I stopped at the bank and from there I went to the Hospital.

"He never regained consciousness, and died three days ago." said a nurse.

I left the hospital feeling dazed and unsure of what to do next. I did not know where he lived, I had never met his relatives and now I had missed his funeral.

Press releases from the company later on confirmed twenty four dead, countless injured and five missing. But according to company officials, "There were many alive, thanks to the safety procedures in place at the time of the incident. Those lucky ones are still with their friends and families."

I read the article on the newspaper and I had to sit down. A homeless clutching a brown bag, oblivious to his surroundings, slept in the next bench. I stood there for a long time watching a lonely cloud in the blue sky.

Maybe Billy Bones was one of the lucky ones. He had finally quit, escaped and was now with his friends and family.

His countdown had finally stopped.

THE ONE THAT
GOT AWAY

"Open up. This is the police!" There was rustling and scrambling from the lower bunk bed.

"Gino, Gino." Max was whispering and shaking my bed.

I woke up. "What the hell is happening?" It was pitch dark.

"I have no idea." There was more knocking and another voice said. "Max, we need everybody in the gym immediately."

"Even Mr. C. is here." I climbed down. "Something big must be going on."

"Yeah" Max sounded worried. "But why are the police here?"

"There is only one way to find out."

We came out and joined other students rushing through the hallway, some halfway dressed but most in pajamas. Uniformed police officers guarded already closed doors.

The gym was the largest area close to the dorm. When we got there, throngs of noisy students were filling the bleachers and others were lining up against the wall. The question on everybody's mind was. "What happened?"

We didn't have to wait very long before Mr. C. came out of the Administrative Office followed by a uniformed cop and another older man in civilian garb.

"I apologize for the inconvenience this may cause but we have a most grave situation." He paused and surveyed the group.

There was total silence.

"Last night there was a break in and a large sum of money was taken from the Recording Studio Offices." He paused to let it sink in.

A buzz of ohhs! And ahhs! rose up from the now fully awoken students and a clamoring of voices soon overpowered the Director's speech.

Max was looking at me and his jaw dropped. I must have had the same expression. He quickly looked around. "Where the hell is Brandon?" I was wondering the same thing.

"Or KC" I added immediately. The Director was raising his hands to appease the crowd until it got quiet again. "That's why the police are here to help in the investigation. The Institute, as all of you are well aware, has the right to search your rooms if there is an imperative reason to do so. Today, we have no choice but to act on behalf of your safety. Your rooms are being inspected as we speak."

Again the clamor went up a notch and some protesters raised their fists claiming their right to privacy. Mr. C. had to labor longer to pacify the crowd. "We are not in any way targeting a single individual, all rooms are being inspected. However, if you have any information..."

Max and I were busy looking among the crowd that had started to move. "...remain where you are until you are allowed to return to your rooms..." The director was saying over the students garble.

"Brandon! Right there!" I tagged at Max. Across the room Brandon was trying to hide behind the crowd. He must have seen us because he bolted down the hallway, but was blocked by two cops and returned to reception.

"...and you must sign next to your name on the list." The director was saying. We joined the line forming and approached Brandon. "What the hell happened? Where is KC?" We were talking at the same time.

"I don't know. I have no idea." We could tell he was lying.

We had scanned the crowd and now we were sure KC was not here.

We waited in line to sign the student list. Max was grinding his teeth. "Why he had to screw it up, I had it all planned down to the last detail." He said in a whisper.

Brandon and I agreed.

It had all started about two weeks before. On that particular day, after class, I wasn't feeling well. A splitting headache was killing me. I usually stayed late at the library where I did most of my homework and did all my reading. Today, however, I stopped at the first aid office, got a couple of pain killers and headed to my room.

This was my first year at The Institute and I was sharing the room with a senior student named Max. Max in the lower bed enjoyed waking me up by kicking my butt under the mattress. The higher I bounced the louder he laughed. Later on, he stopped doing it when I pretended I enjoyed it. He was in his early twenties and he was graduating this school year. Max had been working for the Institute for the last three years and gained enough trust from Mr. C. the Institute Director, that he had been appointed his assistant.

Max was in charge, among other things, of transporting the money from the other three branches around the city and suburbs to headquarters, our location. He did this and other chores that involved a lot of inside information.

I was flattened on my bed covered from head to toe and just barely falling asleep when the door slammed open, but I didn't move.

Max and the rustle of two more pairs of feet came through the door.

"C'mon guys. Brandon, close the door." Max said as he sat on his bed, then almost in a whisper. "What I am about to tell you can make us very rich. But not a single word leaves this room. You must keep your mouth shut. KC, especially you, watch what you say around your stupid friends."

"You're my friend too." KC said, with that permanent half twitch of a smile.

KC and his baby face seemed to be grinning or about to say something silly all the time. And then he usually did. He wore a baseball cap pointing the wrong way, which he considered to be extremely cool. He was taken as some kind of sidekick around older students. Some considered him more like a pet, but a pesky one. Nobody seemed to know why he was there in the first place. At fifteen he was too young to be in college, and he always seemed to be tagging along with the troublemakers.

"Don't try to get smart with me KC." Max's tone was now serious. "If you're here it is because we want to help you, but you have to do exactly what I tell you, OK?"

"You're the boss Max."

"Got that Brandon?"

"Whatever you say Max" Brandon said eagerly, trying to please.

Brandon was the classic nerd, with more pens in his shirt pocket than he would ever need. He wore rimmed glasses and a permanent scruffy look. He was a junior and was taking advanced computer classes.

Whenever one of us, in the "Introduction to Computers," class had a question, after class, we knew who to ask. Brandon was a permanent fixture in the computer lab with Help Desk in Information Technology.

Right off the bat, I smelled trouble. The meeting of these characters was suspicious. So I kept quiet on my top bunk bed and listened.

"Every Friday," Max started. "I bring the money from the Englewood Branch. I usually turn the money over to Mr. C's office on the third floor. Other people from the other two branches do the same. He waits until all is there to count it. Makes a report then locks it in the safe. Sometimes if one of the branches is late he just leaves it on his desk and the following day takes it to the Bank." He paused to let it sink in.

"So, the money stays here for one night." Brandon said as if thinking out loud. "But, do you have the safe's combination?"

"Not exactly, but that's where you come in." Max said, playing the ringleader's role to the hilt.

"Sorry Max, but I'm not a safe cracker."

"You don't have to, Brandon. Next week, all you have to do is remove Mr. C's computer from his office for repair and I'll take care of the rest." Max seemed reluctant to give all the details.

"What if the computer is not broken?" Brandon puzzled.

"Don't worry. I'll make sure it is broken." Max said matter of fact.

"So you think the safe's combination is in the computer and you want me to crack his password, access his user profile, hack the SAM files and find the secret code? I imagined Brandon rubbing his hands in anticipation.

"No, all I want you to tell Mr. C. is that it would take at least two days to get the computer fixed." Max saw Brandon's bewilderment.

"OK. Here is why. Whenever his computer is broken he uses the other computer in the studio, he leaves the connecting door to his office open. I have a key for the studio but not for his office. Get it?"

"Oh, OK." Brandon said somewhat still puzzled.

"When the money is late AND his computer is broken the money is there on his desk accessible from the studio. Now you see the connection?"

"OK, I got it."

"I don't get it." KC piped in. "Can you go over it again..."

"You don't have to understand this part KC." Max smiled. "Your job is going to be more fun." He pulled a piece of paper and drew a figure.

"See this? It's the third floor. I have a key for door one, door two, but not for door three. I have a key for door four which is the Studio. The secretary's office is door three, which is open during the day, but she locks it when she leaves. In the back of her office there is a door that is always unlocked; it opens to a hallway where one end goes to the Studio and the other leads to a bathroom. This bathroom has a window that opens to the parking lot." He paused to regain his breath. "You follow me?"

"I think I got lost around door two." KC said unashamed.

Max took a deep breath. "Don't worry, that's not important either." He drew more on the paper. "Two weeks from now your job will be to climb down from the roof to this bathroom window. Go in through the bathroom and down the hallway. The second door on the right is the secretary's door, this door is unlocked, go in and open the front door. I will be waiting for you right there. Then you go down the stairway and go to your room."

"Are you out of your mind? I am not going to climb from the roof three floors above ground..."

"Shhh, keep it down. You are going to be secured from above by a cable and harness. Brandon is going to help you on the roof. Once you are in, he is going to retrieve the rope and head down to the lockers I'll meet him there."

"Can we get a key for that door in between?" Brandon said, "that way nobody has to climb down from outside to open that door."

Max was reluctant to go on about the details but he finally said. "The answer is no. I can't get a key, I tried. But the purpose is twofold, because coming from outside it will point to a thief breaking in. Get it?"

"Wow! You're a genius." KC lit up.

"The only problem," Brandon said "is that the security guard on the first floor may see us on the roof or may see KC climbing down."

A flurry of questions and doubts came from KC and Brandon, now they were smoking and the thick clouds were filling the room. For several minutes I fought to contain a sneeze, but it was too much.

"Achuuu" I exploded.

"What the..." Max jumped out.

I sat up faking an exaggerated yawning. "Oh man, I was passed out. Hey guys! I didn't know you were here." They were looking at each other in disbelief. Another yawn and I dropped back on my pillow pulling the sheets over my head.

"Get your ass down here, NOW." Max screamed and kicked my mattress. I was catapulted out of the bed and landed on my butt.

"You did hear what we were talking about, RIGHT?" He was clearly pissed.

"No, I swear. I was sound asleep." I didn't sound very convincing.

After some bickering that went back and forth, Brandon seemed ashamed and wanted to leave, but Max made him stay. KC was cursing left and right. In the end Max imposing his authority said. "Look maybe he can help us because we may need two guys up on the roof to help swing KC."

"I don't want to be part of anything. Please, I haven't seen or heard anything." I lunged for the door.

Max had me by the shirt in no time and dragged me back into the room.

"Don't be stupid." He said. "You are part of this whether you like it or not." He threw me on the bed. "We may even give you something, huh?" He looked at the other two.

After some weak protests from KC, They all agree I could join the group, and I had no choice but to follow along.

Max went over the plan again and I even suggested using the trash chute to get rid of the rope, harness or any incriminating evidence without leaving the building. The trash chute led straight to the dumpster in the parking lot. Everybody thought this was a good idea.

"How much money are we talking about." Brandon wanted to know.

Max thought for a little bit. "I would say about $10,000 dollars each." KC was rubbing his hands.

"So, we have two weeks to prepare. The day is not this coming Friday, but the next. Everybody got that?"

We did.

The following day Max and I went with KC to check out the roof to find a solid point to tie the rope.

"You must be out of your freaking mind if you want me to go down there!" KC was terrified when he looked over the edge and admitted he was afraid of heights. Max looked at me and pointed his thumb down.

Later when we were alone Max said. "That's the only reason he was part of the group. If he can't do that he's out." He turned. "Do you think you can do it?"

I thought for a little bit. "I think I can."

Max did not dismiss KC right away. We all pretended he was still part of the group but we went to great lengths to keep important information from him.

Four days later Max had the rope ready in the storage room. We met a couple more times during the week to polish some details. KC was suddenly more interested in other details and Max had to tell him several times that he had it under control.

"Why do you want to know at what time the secretary leaves? That does not affect the plan KC. Don't worry about it." Max would patiently say.

"Yea but, you know. I just want to help..." Maybe he suspected something.

Later that day we met again, however KC was nowhere to be found. "Today is Friday." Max said. "I'm just double checking everything. I'm bringing the money a little late just to make sure Mr. C. still leaves it in his desk. I just wanted to tell you that KC is out for good. I haven't told him anything yet but I will."

Now, that had been yesterday.

Today, Saturday morning we were shocked to find out that we had a break in and the gossip was that more than $100,000 dollars in cash had been stolen from the Recording Studio on the third floor.

"That's not right." Max whispered. "We never collected that much."

After a while a uniformed police officer joined the Institute Director and the two detectives by the podium.

"You may return to your rooms. But nobody is allowed to leave the premises for the time being." The Director announced on the PA system.

Brandon wanted to take off, but some convincing made it clear that it was in his best interest to talk. Once back in our room he started to sing.

"I didn't want to do it." He was almost crying.

"Where the hell is KC?" Max was shaking Brandon really hard.

"He was supposed to be here, but he's gone, I swear it was his idea." Max and I exchanged knowing looks.

"You mean you helped KC do the hit one week before our planned date? Were you going to split the loot and leave us out to dry? Huh?" Max was getting really pissed off.

"It was his idea. He said we could do it without you and Gino. But I didn't get any money. I swear."

"He tricked you into helping him and he left with the money right?" Max said almost laughing.

"Yeah, I waited in the stairway for about an hour, when he didn't show up I came back here and he was gone." Brandon's eyes were wide open.

Max and I didn't know whether to be mad or laugh at the same time. KC had tricked us all. How was it possible that the youngest of all had outsmarted Max? A week before the planned date, KC was gone and so was the loot. He had done it himself.

"The son of a bitch! Bastard sucker, traitor!" Max was clearly pissed off.

"Let's check his room" I said still unconvinced.

"Cops already did" Max said scratching his head.

Rapid knocking on the door made us jump. "Max. Are you in there?" Mr. C's booming voice thundered in the hallway.

"Yes. I'm coming." Max casually answered. But his jaw was halfway open.

"What are we going to do now?" Brandon was whispering and clearly shaken.

"Nothing we haven't done anything wrong. If he is the only one missing he is the one with the money. You don't know anything. We never planned anything. OK?" Max opened the door and followed Mr. C. to his office where we later learned was interrogated extensively.

The only one missing and whose whereabouts were unknown was KC. According to the rumor mill, he had hidden in Mr. C's office early that day. In the evening when Mr. C. left, KC simply picked up the money and walked out. Doors 3 and 2 opened from inside. The problem was door one, that had to be opened from the outside. Brandon was to open it at a prescribed time, then go and wait in his room for KC. The security guard had not seen anybody leaving the building. KC had used the trash chute to escape, landed in the dumpster and disappeared.

During the following days most of us were interviewed but nobody had any knowledge of KC's actions or who may have helped him. We said that we were convinced he had worked alone. And, no we had no idea where he might be, after all we hardly knew the guy.

KC had disappeared into thin air.

The following week we all left for vacation. Max left for good and I never saw him again. Brandon and I returned the following school year and although we ran into each other often times, we never discussed the subject.

The Institute never disclosed the amount of money stolen and Mr. C. resigned shortly after the incident for reasons unknown. The rumor was that he was being investigated for misappropriation of funds. KC had used us to do what he did, but now I wasn't too sure. Who had used who to steal how much?

THE MIRAGE OF THE FAR EAST

The 747 broke through the clouds. Right below us, the mountains were closing fast. The entire horizon was blocked by high peaks covered by lush tropical forest. Out of the trees sprung modern glass buildings and manicured mansions, hanging for dear life on the steep slopes. The airplane banked to the right, straining to its limits its superstructure. Trees and buildings, now at a weird angle moved slowly just beyond arm's reach. Shaking and jolting, now sinking, then rising, finally steadying itself it lined up with the runway.

"Welcome to Kai Tak, Hong Kong's International Airport, this is your captain speaking..."

"Oh man, I can't believe we're here." Anthony smiled punching me on the shoulder.

The airplane had come to a stop and some passengers were already pulling their bags from the overhead compartments.

"I think we'd better hurry up, we have too many things to do." I said as a reminder to my companion that this was not a pleasure trip.

We had exactly four hours before our meeting with the sales manager from Cathay International LTD an Import/Export company in the industrial area of the North Territories.

"To The Old Astor" I said as we boarded the taxicab.

After taking a shower and dressing appropriately for a business meeting we made a call.

"I am glad you are already here, but no, you don't need to come to our main plant. We have an office right there in Kowloon." Mr. Chang said on the other side of the line. We penned down the new address and off we went.

The streets were crowded with tourists, businessmen, and vendors. Tiny shops with narrow entrances seemed to have been squeezed and the merchandise was overflowing to the sidewalk. Our destination led us into a deceiving small shop, however, once inside there were more shops and farther down spacious offices.

On the door, engraved in brass, was the name of the company in the two official languages; Mandarin and English. The office itself was small but the side glass walls made it feel much bigger and at the same time it let the customer see the adjacent show rooms that displayed the thousands of products the company dealt with. We introduced ourselves to the two men in business suits. "Yes, I spoke with you on the phone. I am Mr. Chang and this is my associate Ed the sales manager." The older man behind the desk said shaking our hands with a slight head bow.

"We have the product you requested and we consider it to fit your specifications." The sales manager said in a solemn tone as he handed me a rectangular black object.

I released the latch mechanism and opened the spring loaded cover, checked roll pins and hub leaf spring.

"Grade A," the sales manager said, as if that would stop me from continuing my inspection.

There was not much I could conclude then until I took it apart and inspected every single part of it, reassemble it and run it through rigorous tests. I snapped the cover shut and it locked in place with a solid click.

I pushed it back on the table towards the sales manager. All eyes were watching my moves.

"We will need at least three samples for testing and it will take us at least two days to complete it, at that time we will let you know if we move forward." I said in a detached and unemotional voice, looking straight at Mr. Chang.

"But..." The sales manager started.

"That's fine," the old man cut in, his open hand in the manager's direction. "I don't see any problem. We want you to be comfortable with our product."

He turned to the sales manager and spoke fast and briefly in a lower voice in Mandarin. The sales manager got up and left the room. Now all smiles, Mr. Chang turned to us. "He is bringing up your samples; in the mean time I'd like you to see our line of products."

We followed him to the show rooms. There on swinging displays, walls and tables, were toys, all kinds of clothing, fine silks, T-shirts, tools, medical supplies, and piled on a table were catalogs with more items. He also said that they could mass produce any plastic part made to specs.

We left with the samples in our briefcases and it was not until we were back in our room that we felt more at easy to talk.

"So what do you think" said Anthony.

"Well it looks like they run a big operation, big company."

"I mean the tapes," he said pointing to the brief cases.

"Well, let's take them apart."

I took the black VHS tapes out of the briefcase, went to my luggage and got a Philips screwdriver. Thirty minutes later I had inspected every individual part and reassembled all three video tapes. No question about it: grade A. Now the second phase of the mission was the actual recording testing. It was late in the afternoon, with video recording camera in hand we headed to Victoria Harbor for some sightseeing.

"Hey, why don't we try that Chinese restaurant" I said to Anthony, after some heavy recording.

"They're all Chinese." He said smiling.

"Okay, you got me."

Later, back at our Hotel, we pulled our VCR from our luggage and played back the tape to check picture quality. We replayed and re-recorded small sections at random to check for picture degradation, no problems found.

The following day we were ready for more exhaustive work of sightseeing, this time it was Victoria Peak. The Ferry took us across Victoria Harbor to the Hong Kong Island. The Peak, as it is locally known, offers one of the most astounding and spectacular views of the city. For our video recording testing, it was just unbeatable.

"You know what? I hate that we have to erase the video tapes to keep testing." Said Anthony as we munched on delicious clams at one of the many fine restaurants crowded with tourists, as our video camera whirred rewinding the tape.

"Who cares? We can return here any time! We're going to be rich, filthy rich!" I said imagining the huge profits on the most amazing deal we were working on.

"That is, of course, if we close the contract."

"Of course we're going to close the contract, I don't see any problem so far, do you?"

The Contract, yes, after weeks of negotiations through phone conversations, letters and faxes we had agreed on price per item, provided we bought a minimum quantity. All this had not been easy. We had to provide letters of intent from our Bank to their Company and other paperwork just to get things going. The video recording testing, more than just a formality, was our insurance that we were getting a quality product for our customers back in The Philippines.

"If you say so, you're the tape expert." He said digging into the main course.

Anthony was more reserved on the idea of getting rich, perhaps because he already was, or more accurately, his father was. His family had been for generations one of the largest landowners just north of Manila. They owned extensive coconut and sugar cane plantations, farms for swine breeding and other industrial investments. I had met Anthony in Chicago when we both worked for the same Company, although he was part of the office staff in the Data Entry and I in the manufacturing floor, we hit it off right from the get go because we were both attending the same Chess tournaments and loved to play the game.

One day the Company announced it was closing for good. One by one, the employees were called to the office, there; the Company Official laid it out on the table.

"You've been with the Company for four years." The Official said when it was my turn. "We are offering you 3,000 dollars per year, plus our matching contribution to your 401K, the total comes to thirty one thousand four hundred and twenty dollars. What do you think?"

What did I think? This was more money than I had ever had or seen in my whole life! Did I have a choice? I'd better take it before they changed their minds.

"Well...Okay." I was speechless.

"I need you to sign here for me. We truly appreciate your time with us and we wish you good luck." He handed me a copy of my voluntary resignation and a crisp check worth a fortune.

Anthony had received a similar amount and the following day he had friends and relatives over to celebrate.

"What are you going to do now?" he asked.

"I have no Idea." I was young, single, no attachments, no family.

"What about you?" He had a wife and two kids.

"My wife wants to go back to the Philippines. She's tired of the cold, the snow. You know."

"But, what are you going to do over there."

"There's plenty to do." He sounded upbeat. "I, for one, want to get into politics. I have the contacts, I know a lot of people, and my father has some powerful and influential friends in the Government."

"Wow! That sounds like a fun and exciting thing to do."

"You bet." It sounded like he had already made up his mind.

"Why don't you come with me?" He said out of the blue.

"Me?" It did sound like an adventure, but politics was definitely out of my league.

"There are a lot of business opportunities over there." He said excitedly.

"Mmm, I don't know. When do you leave?"

The first month or so in the Philippines had been nothing but welcome parties, celebrations, cookouts, the beaches, nightclubs, unlimited San Miguel's and Don Pedro Rum. By the second month when our heads cleared a little, during one of our trips to Manila I noticed how expensive a regular T-120 VHS blank tape was.

"Can you believe they want ten dollars for a blank tape?" I told Anthony.

"They have to import them from Taiwan, Korea or Japan." He said matter of fact.

"Still, it's a rip-off. You know how much it costs to make one? Seventy five cents."

"How much are they in The States?"

"Retail, six to eight dollars."

"Well, somebody is making a big bundle."

"Are you thinking what I'm thinking?" I could see dollar signs in his eyes.

For the next couple of weeks we did some research on the retail market. We found that most retailers were paying six or more dollars per tape unit, how much more they would not say but one thing was for certain: they would buy from us at five dollars per unit. Next, we pored over merchandise catalogs, import, export agencies and Companies based in Singapore, Hong Kong, Korea, Japan and, Taiwan. Finally deciding for Hong Kong when they offered a price we could not refuse.

Anthony had been on the phone for quite a while bargaining the price for 10,000 units. When he finally hung up, he was smiling ear to ear. "I think we got it, I think we got it."

"Got what?"

"We got them for a dollar a piece!" This was way beyond what we had expected.

I was already doing mental calculations. "O.K. 10,000 dollars plus shipping plus..."

"There is a little problem." He cut my train of thought.

"We have to buy a minimum of 50,000 units" my jaw dropped to the floor.

"50,000! That's a lot! I wanted to start small, how much for 10,000 units?"

"Anything less than 50,000 is two dollars apiece."

We discussed the pros and cons. Even if we bought 10,000 units at two dollars apiece, after expenses we would still make about 20,000 dollars which was a pretty decent profit. But, if we bought 50,000 our profits would jump to over 150,000 dollars, considering that the shipping cost was the same for either quantity.

"There's no question about it, the 50,000 units is the best deal." Anthony said after adding overhead, distribution, transportation, labor, etc.

"I agree, let's go for it."

Earlier we had agreed to a 50/50 partnership and by going with this deal we had to put everything we had.

We immediately went to the proper government offices and registered an Import /Export Corporation of which we promptly made ourselves President and vice president.

Armed with quality business cards we returned to those retailers that had expressed interest. Soon, we had their intent to buy from us and the amount of units, which wasn't really more than a few hundred, but it was a start.

Now, that we were here in Hong Kong and almost done testing the sample tapes, we were pretty confident we had everything under control.

"We really don't have to do a lot more testing. Let's re-record one more tape and watch it later. Then, tomorrow morning we can call Mr. Chang to meet with them." I told Anthony.

"Sounds good to me," he was absorbed ogling a stunning red head walking past our table.

The following day we called Mr. Chang to set up a meeting and sign the contract. At the indicated time, we arrived at the office, only this time the sales manager had been replaced by another old man with somber attitude and dressed completely in black.

"Please meet Mr. Ling our Financial Officer," said Mr. Chang glancing at the Undertaker.

We shook hands and as we sat at the desk Mr. Chang moved a stack of documents in our direction.

"These are the contract documents."

"Jesus," I thought. "We just want to buy some tapes, not the entire Company."

"You do not have to sign it right now, feel free to read it and let us know if you have any questions." The undertaker piped in. His English was almost perfect. "However, we can review the main points." He added.

In no time we were just signing on the dotted line. He would pick two or three pages at a time and say "Oh, this is just... da, da, da," suddenly his English wasn't so good, then he would end up with a clear. "Sign here."

After agreeing to a lot of "da, da, das," we were off to the Bank to sign an affidavit confirming the wire transfer from our Bank to theirs. Fifty percent of total payment immediately and the balance upon merchandise delivered in Manila Harbor in two weeks' time. We shook hands and we went our separate ways.

We stayed in Hong Kong one more day visiting The Floating Restaurants and The Zoo among others.

Two weeks later: Manila, Philippines.

"Container just arrived at the warehouse!" Anthony shouted on the phone.

"Thank God! It was about time." The late delivery, according to Mr. Chang, was due to Typhoon Watch in The South China Sea, holding the ships at Bay.

"Good, I'm rounding up the guys to unload it." We had rented a small office in downtown Manila with a warehouse in the back. First order of the day had been to fix the window Air Conditioned and buy fans for the warehouse.

According to the locals, this summer was hotter than previous years. For the last week or two we had over one hundred degrees in the shade.

From the day we returned from Hong Kong, we had been a flurry of activity from forming a group of salesmen, having vehicles available for delivery, ordering forms, getting orders, to buying office equipment, it was one of those "hurry-up-and-wait" situations, but finally we were ready to take off.

The following day we made our first delivery.

"I can't believe we're actually doing it." I said waiving our first payment. "We're rich! We're rich!"

After all these weeks of waiting it had been nerve wrecking, just thinking what could go wrong and lots of what if's. After all, we had everything riding on this deal. Thank goodness all we had to do now was to concentrate making the sales.

Then the first call came in.

I could not believe what my customer was saying on the other end of the line. "No, that's impossible. Maybe they're not ours. Can you double check again?"

I ran to the warehouse, where Anthony and the others were packing boxes. "Stop, Stop! We have some bad tapes!" I grabbed a handful of tapes and started frantically disassembling them.

"Bad, like, in broken?" Anthony wasn't concerned, but I had my suspicions.

"Not exactly, according to our customer, the tape starts running fine, but after a little while the tape just unwinds out of control and jams the head mechanism." After a few minutes I had all the pieces exposed, and my suspicions were confirmed.

I must have looked like a ghost.

"What? What is it?" Anthony was starting to worry.

"We have to check at least one tape from every box." I said, still hoping for a miracle.

I picked a piece of plastic from the bottom of the tape. "See this? This is called a pressure flap. Grade A tapes have this flap welded by Ultrasound." I rubbed my fingers on the sticky flap. "This is glue!"

"But, we... I mean, you checked the samples, right?"

"Yes, and they were grade fucking A!"

"Maybe not all are bad, maybe..." now he was running around, his hands up in the air. Suddenly I felt sick. I had a sinking feeling of what we were going to find in every single tape.

"The bastards! Let's get the Chang's on the phone!" Now I was really mad.

"We are not responsible how you handle the merchandise." Mr. Chang said on the other side of the line.

"It's got nothing to do with how we handle the merchandise! You sent us a substandard product. Not the one we paid for." He was trying to avoid responsibility.

After more heated exchanges I was fuming and he just hung up.

"Hey, Anthony do you know any good lawyer?"

He did.

The offices of Albert Grijalva and Associates were on the third floor of a high-rise in the affluent Makati suburb just south of the Pasig River. An attractive Mestiza on the front desk directed us to a spacious office with paneled walls and leather backed chairs.

"Mr. Grijalva will be with you in a few minutes," her winning smile showing the whitest teeth.

Our contract with Cathay International had been delivered to Mr. Grijalva's office three days ago so he could review it, now he was going to advise us how to proceed.

"Magandang umaga po." He said as he entered.

"Good morning." I answered politely. He then exchanged some Tagalog with Anthony. From which I understood that we preferred English.

"There are quite a few clauses that you signed that do not leave much room to contest a claim." He said after leafing through the pages.

I turned to Anthony *"This is just da, da, da, sign here,* remember?"

"I'm sorry?" Mr. Grijalva blinked.

"Nothing, please proceed."

"Your contract with Wong Enterprises LTD..."

"What?" We looked at each other.

"...Releases Cathay International, whose function is only as representative, of any wrongdoing and liability... hence forth..." We were sinking in those chairs, our hopes vanishing into thin air.

"Wong Enterprises LTD is a commercial conglomerate of Mainland China in the Guizhou-Hunan Province..." He continued, switching from obscure legalese lingo into a more understandable Chinese.

"In fact, this is the real contract where you agree to buy 50,000 VHS recording cassette tapes from Wong Enterprises LTD "as is" and there is no mention of grade A." He picked two single pages from the stack and laid them in front of us.

"But..." we didn't even want to see it.

"Yes, everything else is disclaimers and..."

"Wait! We have the sample tapes to prove they lied to us!" Anthony said reaching for our briefcase, ready to pull the undisputable evidence.

"I clearly remember signing a document that stated grade A tapes." I was already standing up and pointing to the rest of the dreadful contract.

"Yes, I even remember the sales manager mentioned grade A." Anthony piped in.

Mr. Grijalva hadn't lost his composure. Slowly he peeled several pages from the stack. "You mean these?" he said as he handed them out.

I was already feeling sick. Mr. Grijalva's expression said it all.

I read it out loud. "Cathay International agrees to supply grade A VHS-T-120 recording cassettes samples FOR TESTING and...As requested per customer." I moved to next page. "Customer found samples to be free of defects..." I stopped flipping through the remaining pages.

"You got to be kidding me!" I said clenching the useless pages. Anthony was holding the two open tapes.

"I am sorry." Mr. Grijalva said standing up slowly. "I wish I could help you, but there is nothing I can do."

"How about a lawyer in Hong Kong, could they do something? We didn't want to give up.

"I doubt it, there is no official Diplomatic Relations with Communist China, ten years from now Hong Kong will revert back to China but for now tensions remain high." He did seem concerned of our plight.

"What do you suggest we do?" We were pulling at straws.

"Call Mr. Chang and ask him in good faith to understand your problem, maybe he can do something." I knew we were doomed.

"Salamat po." I said shaking his hand as we were leaving. Anthony stayed behind a little conversing in rapid fire Tagalog.

We headed back to the office. The sun was blasting down in all its fury. The diesel fumes from the traffic were overpowering. Multicolored jeepneys whizzed by overflowing with passengers that held for dear life on the edge of the open doors.

"You know what?"

"What?"

"One day I'm going to write a book and write about our misfortunes."

"What are you going to call it?"

"I don't know. Something like, *How to lose 50,000 dollars without really trying.*"

"Not bad. It sure beats, *Two Stupids Abroad.*"

"What are we going to do now?" I asked Anthony once we were back next to the mountain of ripped open boxes.

"Call Mr. Chang, I guess." His ten fingers were sliding down his face that looked longer than it was.

"I guess it's your turn because after I yelled and screamed at him I don't think he wants to talk to me." I knew I would not be able to plead and beg when in reality I wanted to strangle him.

After several failed attempts to get through we finally had a secretary supposedly trying to locate him. She came back saying that he was not available, but she said to call the following day.

We did and Anthony begged and pleaded. Mr. Chang mentioned that the tapes were supposed to be in a controlled environment and not baking in more than one hundred degrees. "Well, too late for that" I thought, I was sure they were already cooked before we got them. Anthony was holding me at bay.

"We have nothing to do with the Company in China, and there is nothing we can do. We do not have your money. Your payment was directly to that Company." He sounded apologetic.

"So what do you suggest we do?"

"You could go and talk to the Company in China."

"Are you or a representative from your Company coming with us?"

"We cannot offer you a lot of assistance, but we can have a translator accompany you."

"Can we call you tomorrow and let you know if we can do this?"

He agreed and we were there wondering what we were getting ourselves into. We discussed it and we decided we had to find out more information.

"What can I do for you gentlemen?" A tall and soft spoken middle aged man said from behind the desk. A British flag stood to the side and in the back wall in bronze letters said "Manila British Embassy." After giving him the short version of events he said. "You are indeed in a most dire situation and I would not recommend any incursion of the sort you are planning."

"So, you don't think it is a good idea..."

"Our Diplomatic Relations with China are extremely constrained at best. I am sure our Hong Kong office could explain it better, but I understand we had quite a few incidents where Westerners have gone missing or simply disappeared. I am sorry for your financial loss, I am sure it is quite traumatic, but I strongly advise you to think seriously before making any rush decision." We shook hands and left.

We called Mr. Chang and explained we had decided not to pursue the case any further. He sounded even more apologetic and he said he understood the restrictions on foreigners to enter China. "But we could smuggle you across the border in one of our company owned helicopters." He said.

"What?" this sounded too outlandish, but it did sound like fun.

"The only thing is that once on the other side you will be on your own, and if you get caught we heard that The Red Army is not nice."

"Thank you Mr. Chang we appreciate your concern, but we have to decline your offer." Anthony said calmly. I hung up the extension I was listening in to the conversation and now I was thinking really hard. Anthony was still with the phone glued to his ear.

"Wait, I want to go!" I said raising my hand.

"Hold on Mr. Chang we have a volunteer that wants to battle The Red Army!" he said into the phone.

He turned to me, "are you freaking nuts?" he whispered.

I peeled the phone from his ear. "Yes Mr. Chang... Mr. Chang?" only the continuous dial tone was on the line.

"Catch me if you can!" Anthony was already aiming for the door in fake slow motion.

"Bastard! I'll get cha!"

Five days later two trucks, from a plastic recycling company, came to pick up 50,000 useless VHS tapes sold as plastic scrap, and painful as it was to see them being dumped as trash we just wanted to put it all behind us. We had cried, banged on the walls and believe it or not we even had tried to repair and re-glue the pressure flaps to no avail.

Having lost everything I had, it was time for me to return to The States. Anthony's family had been good to me and wanted me to stay. Teary eyed I hugged them and said. "Nagpapasalamat po ako sa inyong napalakalaking tulong sa amin."

"Don't mention it." Anthony said. "I'm sure you would've done the same thing for me."

I rode into the sunset, again.